D1347189

EVERY SEVENTH WAVE

TOM VOWLER is an award-winning novelist and short story writer living in the UK. His debut story collection, *The Method*, won the Scott Prize and the Edge Hill Readers' Prize, while his novels *What Lies Within* and *That Dark Remembered Day* received critical acclaim. He is an associate lecturer in creative writing at Plymouth University, where he completed his PhD. His second collection of stories, *Dazzling the Gods*, was published in 2018. More at www.tomvowler.co.uk

ALSO BY TOM VOWLER

NOVELS
What Lies Within
That Dark Remebered Day
Dazzling the Gods

SHORT STORIES
The Method

EVERY SEVENTH WAVE

TOM VOWLER

SALT

CROMER

PUBLISHED BY SALT PUBLISHING 2021

2 4 6 8 10 9 7 5 3 1

Copyright © Tom Vowler 2021

Tom Vowler has asserted his right under the Copyright, Designs and
Patents Act 1988 to be identified as the author of this work.

First published in Great Britain in 2021 by
Salt Publishing Ltd
12 Norwich Road, Cromer, Norfolk NR27 0AX United Kingdom

www.saltpublishing.com

Salt Publishing Limited Reg. No. 5293401

A CIP catalogue record for this book is available from the British Library

ISBN 978 1 78463 239 7 (Paperback edition)
ISBN 978 1 78463 240 3 (Electronic edition)

Typeset in Neacademia by Salt Publishing

Printed and bound in Great Britain by Clays Ltd, Elcograf S.p.A

imo
Felton William Vowler

EVERY SEVENTH WAVE

H E WATCHED FROM an upstairs window as she entered the water. It was one of the few not boarded up, this side of the house defended from stone-throwers by a sheer drop to the rocks below. The room itself was empty these days, save an old rocking chair that had been his mother's, where on occasion he'd observe the cycle of the Atlantic as it pitched and tossed, the wading birds that prospected the strandline. He'd vowed last year to make something of it, return it to the clutch of habitable rooms, but there was comfort found in sparsity, like a meditation.

He supposed it would have been one of the more expensive guest rooms, and he imagined his mother proudly opening the door for visitors, letting the panorama announce itself, the next landfall a barely conceived thing. This time of year, the hill to the west kept the setting sun from the room, right until it breached the horizon, when it would ignite the sky in a kind of performance.

He saw the woman had paused for a moment, glancing back to the shore, before continuing further into the sea and he had to work hard to see her in the dusk.

Like the birds he was not beyond searching the line of wrack himself, a ribbon of detritus, source of endless flotsam: wood for fuel or furniture; a pair of sunglasses he kept though didn't wear. He had found shoes, hot water bottles, skulls of various mammals, all curated by the waves after their immense journeys. A tiny porcelain figurine, which he'd taken home and placed above the fire. Twice a day the sea bestowed him with gifts, objects cleansed and softened before being returned to the land.

And so many dolls. He never understood where all the dolls came from. Or who lost them. He imagined all the others that must be adrift, eddying eternally in orphaned buoyancy. There had been a singular doll's head last week, poised on a heap of desiccating rope, its eyes blinking when he tilted it back and forth, giving it life. Where have you come from, he asked it.

Once a dead seal lay across the seaweed, half its head missing, flank corkscrewed open – a propeller most likely – and for days he watched the gulls and redshanks pick it clean. And last winter, half a mile or so along, there was that time the dog wouldn't give up its find, a severed foot still in its shoe, the dog a primal thing in those moments, letting no one near it. Later the police told him how easily feet detached from a body after a month or more at sea. One of the fishermen lost a few months earlier, they reckoned, and he had imagined a family member summoned to identify the boot, for surely one foot looks much like another, especially after so long in the water. He didn't recall hearing of any more found and wondered what someone did with just a foot.

☙

The light was receding with speed now and he had to adjust his position at the window to follow the woman, could see that the water was up past her knees. She might still turn back, he said to himself. There was no need to do anything yet.

For three successive evenings she had arrived around twilight, looking out to sea, lost to thought, standing a few feet from the cliff edge until darkness claimed her. He'd taken the dog out a while later each time, but there'd been no sign of anyone. He didn't recognise her as someone from the village, reckoned on her being mid-twenties or so, a holidaymaker perhaps, though it wasn't the season. He only used a few rooms and in the absence of lights she would presume the house empty, its tumbledown façade and weather-worn roof, its proximity to the cliff that suggested the sea would one day claim it, which it would. He'd once regarded land as unassailable, the changes it endures too small to witness, giving an illusion of permanence. But he knew the sea's furious power now, which he'd listen to at night as it dragged away a little more of the rock beneath him.

To live on the edge of things, he thought. The meeting of two worlds, a liminal frontier, from known to unknown as land gave way to leagues of nothing but sea and all it had laid claim to. His mother once told him the sea was God's instrument of retribution, but some days you looked out at it and knew it was beyond even God's will.

She was deeper now, the woman. Almost to her waist. The sea wasn't at its coldest this time of year, but could still hit you like a shovel if you weren't used to it. He looked to see if anyone else was present, a dog walker or a lover for whom this spectacle was intended, but if there was the gloom had displaced them. There would perhaps be someone set up fishing further along, but their focus would be narrow, outward looking.

He considered for a moment if the scene was indeed real,

and not a cruel re-enactment of a delusional mind, one still manacled to the past, one spent largely in isolation, his heavy drinking days behind him yet not without their legacy. But there was enough continuity for it to be trusted, he was sure, the dog joining him at the window, sensing the thing.

It was a test then, as everything these days was. Nothing stayed still, although more than anywhere he had found an order to things here, an equilibrium that the woman's nightly presence had begun to threaten. He'd wondered if her evening ritual would become a thing of permanence, a harbinger visited upon him each sundown. But tonight, after an hour or so in stillness, she had climbed down a less sheer spot on the cliff, mislaying her footing a few times. At one point she seemed to lose her nerve, but ascending must have felt equally perilous, and a few minutes later she was on the beach, and even from up here he could sense the change in her. He'd watched as she crossed the shale, limping a little, the gloaming shape of her less distinct by the second, and had he not known of her existence she might have been just another shadow. She'd paused at the water's edge, let the swash encircle her feet, and for a moment he thought the reality of the thing would dissuade her.

But now her stride had this purpose, like a switch was thrown, a decision made. Every few yards she fell, recovered and continued, like the sea was a stallion she couldn't stay on for long. Further and further out, more of her below the water than above now.

And then she was gone.

H E ATTEMPTED TO open the window, to get a clearer look, to call out, but it had long since sealed shut. He tried to calculate where the small ridge was, the sand falling away a couple of feet, how it caught out holidaymakers time and again, a riptide often forming a little beyond this. She would resurface, he was sure, and stagger back to shore, cold and rueful, a learning of sorts. But half a minute passed and the water remained unbroken.

There was anger in him now. This was what happened in the world, people forced their business on you, drew you into their lives whether you wanted it or not. Even here, where he'd cocooned himself from the world, fashioned a life of sorts.

He took the stairs three at a time, the dog getting under his feet, animated at the prospect of some event or other. Outside the wind voiced across the garden, in encouragement or torment he couldn't tell, the briny spray like an ablution. He was halfway through the mob of weeds when he thought of the torch, but that would take another minute, which could be the difference. The dog was barking now, playing some game, trying to herd him, and he shouted it down, felt in himself this great swell of adrenaline.

There was enough light to see the shape of things if not the detail, and he kept a good pace, his body knowing by heart the path's course to the clifftop and a less precipitous route to the beach.

He wondered if she was a good swimmer, whether she'd been drinking. Whether she'd taken a breath before going under. He tried to remember today's high-tide time, calculate what force he would be up against.

His own passage to the beach was more plummet than calculated descent, the gorse-pocked scree slowing his fall only a little. He stood, sensed the injuries were superficial, got his bearings back. The dog had found its own way down and stood at his side, awaiting the next component of the game.

The sea was a hundred yards or so away, distinguished from the beach only by its fluctuating, by a thousand ever-shifting contours. There had been moonlight on previous evenings, but the cloud was dense and unbroken tonight.

The water was cold, even to him, each stride less productive than the last. The dog feigned to follow, and he sensed the conflict in the animal, each salvo ending back on the beach, fear trumping instinct.

His boots were soon small anchors, his jeans already twice their weight as he lunged forward in slow motion, and this image of running in cement not yet dried. Once up to his midriff he stopped, tried to becalm his breathing, knew this to be important. He realised he had no idea where she was, that she could be fifty feet or more away.

He heard the dog barking on the shore, called it to quieten so he could listen for splashes. Less than two minutes, he reckoned he'd been. Even if she'd been under all that time, the temperature might save her, force the blood to vital organs. Slow everything down.

The cold was deep in him now, his body sluggish as it tried to preserve itself. He removed his top, thinking he should have taken everything off on the beach, that the extra time would have been worth it.

He called out several times, felt the immense scale of the water around him, felt his impotence. The fear he once had of water returned, like a half-forgotten lover, and he forced it back down, refused to acknowledge it.

A wave broke on his back, was enough to unbalance him and he took in some water, lost the direction of things for a moment. He had tried, he said to himself. You couldn't stop someone if they were determined. He'd acted with swiftness once he realised, there was no need to berate himself.

She burst through the surface a few yards from him, arms flaying, spluttering out the sea, taking big gulps of air before going under again. He pushed through the water until the seabed fell away and he had to swim, the fear rising again, like an old habit, all the unknown things beneath him.

Feeling down to his laces, he worked them loose, jemmied his boots free as he trod water. He swam for long seconds, but there was nothing when he got to the spot, and he felt with his hands and legs for something solid, his muscles claggy like they were in mud and he knew he'd be of no help soon.

His leg was stuck now, snagged on something, his instinct to kick out, to release himself, but he realised she'd grabbed his ankle, and so he reached down. He held his breath and allowed himself to submerge a little, trying to find something of substance, but if anything she was pulling him further down, further out. A siren, he thought, luring him here, something not of this world.

He managed to surface, could hear the yelp of the dog and he took some big gulps before plunging again, this time

7

forcing his upper body over itself so he could swim down to her. Five, six feet perhaps. He found what he thought must be hair and looped an arm around the mass below it, knowing it was a final effort, that there would be only one go.

He'd read about drowning, of those caught in riptides, the swell and heave of the sea underestimated, the cold sapping all strength from even the strongest. Of boisterous waves that pounded down on you like a ton of gravel until you had nothing left. Fighting it was the mistake, the battering and winding all the worse for it. Soon you couldn't tell up from down, the sea a womb, your senses betraying you. Panic became resignation, the breath held as long as possible but eventually the body disobeyed the mind and breathed for you, the lungs flooding in an instant. Some spoke of euphoria, a painless passing to unconsciousness, but he wondered if this was always the case. Once reconciled to your fate, was it better to inhale deeply, to hasten it all?

It was anger that leavened him, anger that she was drowning them both, and with effort he hadn't summoned before he pulled her up until they were both afloat, their heads almost touching. A pair of buoys bobbing in the mercury water.

He fought the heave and grip of the tide, turning her a little, coiling a forearm around her neck to begin the ungainly swim towards the barking. Several times he felt progress cancelled out as great currents surged them back, and he knew to let them, to concede to its might and start again.

To calm himself he tried to focus on the sky's vastness, let the sough of the breeze revive him. Of all the things to be the unmaking of him, he thought, like it had been scripted. Let go of her and it will be easy, and he wondered perhaps if this was his mother's voice on the wind.

A final push, legs pedalling with all he had, power that was more memory than effort, the muscles all febrile. When finally he could stand, he held her in both arms like a corpse, the sea still reluctant to yield them. He rested her on the water's surface, let himself recover a little.

His legs had no feeling now, his stride coming from some ancient instinct, one after another, each an event. The water receded and he had to take her weight on his own, finding the strength from somewhere, knowing that you could in bursts. Some of the heft of the sea fell from their clothes and as they collapsed on the shingle, the dog yelped and harried, confused at this gift he'd brought them.

Even in the half-light he could see her skin was grey, that the water had claimed its colour, perhaps her life. He fought the shivering and opened her mouth, pushed two fingers in, but it felt clear. He placed an ear to her lips, could hear nothing beyond waves or the dog. Pinching her nose shut he cupped his mouth to hers and blew hard, waited two seconds then blew again. He tried to see if her chest rose, if the instinct to survive was there, and when he couldn't he felt her wrist for a pulse. Don't let this be for nothing, he thought.

He considered shouting for help, knowing even had he the strength to it would be a waste.

He tried to formulate useful thoughts but the cold forbade it. The house was a shapeshifting presence on the cliff and he recalled how twenty minutes ago he had been settling into an unremarkable evening. Longed for it to be this way still.

Do something, he thought. That is better than nothing.

Cupping a fist with his other hand, he knew to press hard, a hundred or so compressions a minute, stopping at thirty to blow into her again, and this time he sensed her chest rise.

9

When she convulsed it wasn't to bring water up but to vomit, the smell a rank thing. Turning her on her side he again forced his fingers into her mouth, scooping the remaining sick out, not thinking about what he was doing, just doing it, and he was glad of the instinct.

The dog had ceased its barking now, the game something sinister, something to fear, and hoping he'd got all the sick out he turned the woman on her back once again. The cloud had parted a little and, her face burnished in moonlight, he got a first sense of what she looked like, saw a waterlogged beauty there.

He was angry again, but different to in the water. Hers was an age when it was all felt so keenly and there seemed no way to go on. An age of absolutes. Nothing is worth this, he wanted to say to her, knowing that sometimes a thing was.

She was completely still, and he could sense death gathering, its leverage almost enough. He leant in and forced more of his air into her, hoping some of it found a way, and then sat back, exhausted, the cold of her lips still on his, the tide behind them an indifferent pulse.

Life was there, he felt, vaporous and fragile but apparent. He wondered what this was based on, whether it was more than hope, more than the need for things to be different this time. He went to continue the resuscitation but spasms of salt water expelled from her lungs, burbling out of her like a blocked drain. She choked and he eased her on her side again, smoothed her back, and the dog resumed its barking.

He was colder than he'd ever been, knew all the effort was futile if he didn't get them to the fire soon. He pictured his boots on the seabed, barrelling out on the tide, and he mourned their loss, as you might a loyal pet. Removing his shirt, he slopped it down, tried to contain the shaking.

Looking up at the house, he thought it possible. She wouldn't be so heavy, even with wet clothes, and after another minute he hoisted her over his shoulder and trudged across the shingle.

THE WHISKY SEARED, its warmth emanating out from the core of him. He worked out the order of things, decided she was OK while he put on dry clothes and saw to the fire. Even if he walked to the village soon, to the phone box, she needed caring for now. He placed a blanket over her, but the wet clothes needed to come off, it was just a fact.

Her breathing was at least regular now, broken only by a steady cough, and he felt sure all the water had come up. When he'd first placed her on the sofa, she was still unconscious and for a minute it seemed he'd lost her after all, her skin sickly blue, the hope he'd had on the beach diminished. What would he do then, he'd thought. But then she'd spluttered some more.

He tried to recall the signs of hypothermia, knew you could recover then relapse. Pneumonia was possible too. Brain damage. Alive is better than dead, though, he told himself.

He removed the blanket and began taking off her jumper, pulling each arm down over her hands, working the thing up over her head as he tilted her towards him. The shirt next, its buttons slipping easily through their holes, its removal revealing a constellation of burn marks on one arm, some healed, others fresh.

Her right flank was adorned with a birthmark, a swarthy terrain, like someone had begun colouring her in but had lost interest. For a moment he was mesmerised, followed it up and down with his eyes, resisting the urge to trace its form with a finger.

She seemed to rouse a little and he thought to stop the undressing, to explain what he was doing, but she drifted away again, between worlds. The shoes were harder, their laces tightly knotted by the water, his fingers too thick, nails bitten too short to get any purchase. He tried to remove a shoe as it was, but these too had contracted, had become part of her. He fetched a small knife and cut each lace below the knot, eased the shoes from her feet, her socks, once removed, like a pair of rats on the floor. He thought he might have to cut the jeans as well, but after initial resistance, they slid down.

He stood back, took in this unfamiliar sight the universe had delivered. Like flotsam. A quick calculation was all it took to recall the last time he'd seen a woman this unclothed. More than a decade, and he tried to remember what intimacy felt like but couldn't. It was as if the body forgot, more than the mind: the brain knew the choreography, its specifics, but not how it felt. She was, he saw now, probably barely twenty, the age his daughter would be.

He told himself to stop thinking, to stay with the order of things.

The fire hadn't caught properly, so he worked on it until the flames bickered and he was sure it would sustain itself. He sidled the sofa nearer the heat, then started to remove her underwear. If she came around he would stop and apologise, hope she remembered what had occurred. That he was helping her.

The order of things, he said to himself.

The pants were skimpy, a vivid pink, and they rolled down her legs until they were just a wet cord, a figure of eight. There was a glimpse of hair, more a tuft, and he stole his gaze from it, distracted himself with the birthmark.

The bra was a deep red, her breasts pushed unnaturally inwards by it. Rather than turn or lift her again, he felt behind her and unclasped it, waiting for her to stir at the embrace but she didn't. Their faces so close, he could smell the whisky on his breath and he was glad he'd got a handle on the drinking. He adjusted each arm in turn and removed the bra, lowered her back down. And then she was naked and something in him did remember an aspect of it all, how it felt.

He sensed her scrawniness was impermanent, like a thing that weighed less than it should, and he wanted to feed her up, remembered the dog when it first arrived, all ribbed and skin-stretched.

Her nakedness was unsettling now, made her somehow more a corpse than a person, and he replaced the blanket. He thought again how life took these turns, how it went from one state to another just when you thought it was stable.

He saw that her left ankle was swollen, probably sprained on the cliff, or turned over in the water. He would put some ice on it soon, bring down the puffiness. Some of the colour had returned to her face and he hoped she was beyond the worst danger. He fetched a towel, patted sections of her hair dry, before propping her head up with a cushion, and there being a sense of accomplishment: perhaps he had saved her, rendered death into life.

The dog watched as he gathered her clothes and crossed the room to arrange them around the fire. Her shoes too. He thought there were some spare laces somewhere and told himself to look later.

He poured another whisky and drank this one slower,

following in his mind the balm as it spread within him, telling himself two was fine. A tonic of sorts. He reckoned on it being around eight o'clock, perhaps a little later, and he tried to remember what plans there had been for the evening, what jobs he'd been minded to attend before all this.

The fire was up now. The wood could last the night if he was careful with it. He'd fetch more when it got light. Turning the armchair out a little, so he could see both the fire and the girl, he let himself fall into it, thinking that if she didn't need checking on, he could happily sleep there until morning.

He thought again about a phone call, at least to report it, but the fire and the whisky were anvils on his shoulders, and it was all he could do just to watch her. There had been a telephone line into the house for the first few years, disconnected when he didn't pay the bill, his parents' old Bakelite handset a thing without purpose now. He should get a mobile. It perhaps cost him work, not having one, but he managed. He would walk to the village first thing, tell someone.

The dog curled at his feet and he envied the animal's easy acceptance of circumstance. A hunger made itself known and he saw it off with the last of the whisky.

It was close to dark in the room when he woke, the fire aglow but silent. Out to sea the lambent sweep from the lighthouse crossed the sky in cadenced relief. There had been a terrible cold in him and he wondered why he wasn't in bed. He half-remembered and looked to the sofa, saw the shape of her, this selkie of the sea, and he replayed it all in his mind.

She was groaning, delirious perhaps, and the noise had been something unfathomable in his dream, sound and images

15

that took him back to adolescence. In the dream he thought he had said: I am done with you.

Still not trusting the scene in front of him, he remained as still as the dog at his feet, waiting until he knew what to do. He felt that despite warming a little, the sea was still in him, its cold grip a diabolical thing. And then he remembered she had been in twice as long as him, had none of his protective fat. The dog the only thing smart enough to stay dry.

He tried to figure out the time from the sky, an hour before dawn perhaps. The hardest part of the day to be awake. He shifted in the chair, the dog grumbling some refrain. He remembered he hadn't got the ice for her ankle, and it took all he had to rise to his feet, his legs protesting. The dog, sensing it wasn't a proper rising, shifted to what was left of the fire.

He put a lamp on and felt her forehead, which was warm but not hot, his touch seeming to quieten her. When he came back from the kitchen she was awake.

H E HELD OUT the ice, which he'd put in a towel.
    Your ankle, he said.

She looked confused but not afraid and he relaxed a little.
You were in the water, he said.

He could see she was thinking about his words, like they were a riddle to be solved, and there was embarrassment in him now, for knowing her intention, for reminding her. She scanned the room and then herself, lifting the blanket a little.

I had to take them off, he said. They were wet. He pointed to where her clothes were drying, neatly arranged and tiny, he thought, like a child's, especially the underwear.

She seemed to accept this, though it was hard to know; he had never been able to tell a woman's thoughts. She pulled the blanket up to her chin, but without panic, looked down at the dog and he hoped the animal was a comfort.

I'll get the fire going in a minute, he said. Are you still cold?

Where am I? she said.

Her accent had a trace of something hard on it, Russian perhaps. He spoke a little slower, a little louder.

In the house on the cliff, he said, along from where you climbed down.

She turned on to her side and winced, touching her ankle while trying to keep the blanket in place.

I don't think it's broken, he said. Sprained, most likely. I

17

have some painkillers. And this. He held out the towel again.

Kneeling at the end of the sofa he asked if she minded and she shook her head. He pushed the blanket back a little. The swelling was no worse than before and he held the ice there gently while she watched.

Can I have some water? she said, her voice faltering, an approximation.

He gestured that the ice was more important.

I can hold it in place with my other leg, she said.

He left and came back with a filled glass and she drank hungrily.

Try to sip it, he said.

He put the box of pills where she could reach them, realised the folly of this, and eased two out from a strip. For the pain, he said.

He wondered again what time it was, how long he'd been in the chair.

Are you hungry? he asked.

She shook her head but then appeared to think about it some more.

A little.

There's some stew.

In the kitchen he saw it was 6 a.m. The tide was back up and he could hear its rhythmic roar, the crash each wave made as it lost stability, the guttural growl when it turned back on itself, raking the shingle. He remembered his boots, how well they fitted, the years they had left in them.

It had been so long since someone else had been in the house, and then not at night, and he didn't know what to make of it. It seemed both unsettling and a kind of relief.

He hadn't felt hungry until he smelt the food, the

microwave turning the portion he'd left for himself last night. He tore some bread off, took it in to her, the dog eyeing him.

Passing her the food, he saw that it didn't work, the mechanics of it, how the towel would fall.

Have you some clothes I can borrow? she said. So I can sit up.

He left the bowl on the coffee table and went up to the bedroom, found the smallest shirt and jumper he had, some socks. He'd wondered what he should bring her to wear on her bottom half, but could think of nothing, so brought down a bigger towel for her to wrap around. After handing them to her, he turned her wet clothes around, moved them closer to the fire, and left her alone. He took some cheese from the fridge, put it on the last of the bread and sat down by the window, the first of the gulls starting up for the day.

He wondered how long he should stay out here, reckoned a few minutes to be sure. It occurred to him that the kitchen was a mess, more than normal, and after eating the bread he put some things away, filled the bin. He thought to put the radio on, to fill the silences, but knew the signal would be weak this time of day. There'd been a television once, that he'd not replaced when it had broken. Again his mind returned to the other time, to his brother choosing the channel when they got home from school, his realising he would always be younger, always behind, and the injustice of this. Their mother fretting about bookings, whether the other rooms would be ready in time. Their big adventure by the sea. And their father, still on board, outwardly committed. He knew memories were sustained if you indulged them, and he tried not to, yet the looping images were so ingrained he had come to accept them.

Outside the living room he coughed to announce himself.

Dawn had arrived imperceptibly, its watery light reviving the room and he guessed they would stay awake now. He cleared away a few things, as if she were a guest, which he supposed she was. He sensed she had dressed, but averted his gaze for now. He fetched some wood and with a little effort the fire returned and he stacked a couple of logs in its centre, the dog now attending to the girl's food.

What sort of dog is that? she asked.

A lurcher, a mix of things.

She looked confused and he thought of the word mongrel, but figured on her not knowing it.

Crossbreed, he said and she nodded.

He saw that she'd eaten some of the food and now gripped the water in both hands. Every now and then she'd clutch her throat and he supposed it was sore from the choking. She looked odd, sitting up in his too big jumper, his woollen socks protruding from under the blanket, and he had to check again whether he was dreaming.

He took the remaining ice and towel away, brought her more water.

Do you want me to call anyone? he said. There's no phone, but I can walk to one.

She shook her head and he thought there was perhaps fear in her eyes for the first time. He'd assumed there would be someone, despite her intentions.

No one in the village? he said.

I do not live here, she said.

Again the accent, which was somehow both barbed and velvety.

The person you're staying with, then?

Another shake of the head. So far he'd only thought about

her physical condition, what damage being in the water might have done.

I can call a doctor in a couple of hours.

My ankle?

Your ankle will heal. I thought someone to talk to.

Shame bloomed in her and he wanted to take it back.

But, yes, he said. A real doctor, to make sure you're OK. Are you in any pain, apart from your ankle?

She said that she wasn't, but that she felt weak.

You can rest here, he said. There's no need to decide yet.

She lay down, seemed content at this. He sat back in the chair and felt the fatigue everywhere, as if some vast gravity was at work, could feel his body, his hair, rimed with salt and sand. He would shower soon.

He tried to think clearly, about what day it was, what the week held. He was due at the yard in a couple of hours, a big order to fill this week. Sixteen skips to weld between the three of them. It was all cash in hand, and nothing if you weren't there. Brutal work, especially in the summer, though he didn't know from one month to the next when he'd be needed. This time of year he could start and finish in the dark, a crepuscular thing. The other two were brothers, their father the yard's owner, so he was only brought in for bigger orders. Between jobs he would go to the village once a week, ring the owner to ask if there was anything.

When not at the yard he maintained a few of the boats in the harbour that belonged to men he'd got to know from fishing, from the pub he sometimes frequented. These were men with sea in their blood, for whom life on land was never entirely trusted, true solitude found only on the water, where a living could still just about be eked out. There was hardship etched in their every feature. Skin inked not in adornment, as it was these days, but from pragmatism, such artwork often the only way to identify a water-dwelling corpse. And their ancestors, sailors who had an image of Christ tattooed on their backs to deter the first-mate taking the whip to them.

Wordless folk, like those he'd known in prison, although these men had their pride still intact. They were tethered to tradition, resisting for now the new order, as the land did the sea, ignoring the reality of fish farms and quotas. Ignoring the knowledge that the sea was being emptied of its crop. For them weather forecasts still hailed from the clouds, from observing the behaviour of seabirds, ancient lore from once Celtic lands. Other boat owners, incomers, had embraced technology, state-of-the-art instruments that could pinpoint shoals of sardines, sonar screens replete with a 70-ton mass. You couldn't compete with that. Some people were just meant for another age, one where you still appeased the gods with garlanded wreaths cast out to sea.

It was the toughest of existences, tougher than the yard. Rising when others were turning in, long days at sea before landing your catch under a gull-bloated sky. Then straight out again, reward a share of the spoils. And yet he understood this, wanted some part of it, the yard a temporary thing, he needed to believe.

Payment for his work – mending nets, painting a hull, removing algae – came with guarded civility, as if he had more in common with the modern fishermen. An outsider, they regarded him, from the family who arrived all that time ago with lavish plans for the big house, plans that crumbled like the rock beneath them. And yet there was an unspoken respect between him and these men, he could sense this. They paid him with cash, a few pints, allowed him to occupy the fringes of their revelry after a good catch, sea shanties filling the night.

He had been told, as every newcomer who arrived at the pub had, of the plague visited upon the village in the seventeenth century, carried by fleas brought in on cloth from London. The material had been damp on arrival, and so was laid out in the square to dry, the fleas dispersing like a virus in all directions. A ravaging and invisible enemy, the plague quickly spread from family to family, announcing itself with swellings on the body, followed by fever and weakness, incredible pain. The skin blackened and bled. In the end death was welcomed.

In an act of selflessness, the people voted to enter a lockdown, nothing coming in or going out until the epidemic had passed, a whole village in quarantine. Church services were held in the open air to reduce the risk of contagion, the dead buried in open land as far away as possible, corpses dragged by loved ones into fields at the edge of the confinement boundary. Despite the seclusion supplies were still needed – food, medicine – so an exchange site was established on the outskirts, goods from the outside world left one week, payment in coins sterilised by vinegar left the next, in a stream for good measure. A year later and more than three-quarters of its population had succumbed, names writ large in the church today. Just ninety-two villagers survived to ensure the community lived on, the sacrifice of those who perished not forgotten. And such solidarity was not diminished by time, its legacy held even today by villagers who still regarded themselves as cocooned from the rest of the country. He liked this even though his own ancestors had been no part of the struggle. Liked that it was remembered. To belong to a place, he thought, that was all we sought.

Once a year out of season the villagers gathered on the beach to bolster the ridge of pebbles that defended their houses from the sea, a half-mile long structure of sea-smoothed stones that depleted a little with each high tide. Potwalloping, he'd heard it termed, and he wondered if the word was used elsewhere. He'd joined them that first year after returning and every one since, an entire morning of backbreaking toil that was both essential and futile, the ridge increasingly a gesture these days as the sea breached it most months. At midday the owner of the pub brought them tots of rum and they would survey their labour with quiet satisfaction.

He noticed the girl was asleep again, her faint snore punctuated by the fire's crackle, so he let his mind stay with the myths of his adopted land.

Less edifying tales were also told, of the coast still possessed by the wraiths of wreckers, folk who profited from a place of serrated reefs and busy shipping routes, the luring of storm-ailed vessels to their demise an industry of its time. It was said some nights, between the keening wind and bawling waves, you could still hear the splintering of wood, the cries of a spilled crew. And the smugglers too, rejecting the duty imposed upon them, shifting contraband from France through labyrinthine tunnels and creep passages that connected churches and inns, supplying a complicit community. Landscape fashioning your vocation. You did what you had to; he had no affection for the law. The sea was both giver and taker of things.

He should like one day to earn a proper living, to know

what was coming in. To buy a boat of his own, run trips to the island or get some lobster pots. Bend the world a little to his own will. There had been a small skiff when he first moved back, abandoned on the beach below, and he'd hauled it up one winter, worked on it in the outbuilding, the project sustaining him, giving him purpose. Once seaworthy he liked to row it out early or late in the day, like some preternatural being, the ocean his alone, and he would tie a baited line to the rowlock, sit back and watch the house as it lost or gained form. He rarely caught anything this way, was content not to but to somehow be bound to the first humans to fish.

HE MUST HAVE dozed, the room full of eager light now, flexing itself like a muscle. Mid-morning, judging by the sun's height, and he cursed another late start at the yard, the grief he would get. The girl was sitting up, examining the painkillers he'd left in error on the table, deciphering the packet's text, though perhaps a shift had occurred in her, the urge to self-destruct receded for now.

Two, he said. And then no more for four hours.

He realised his own head hurt, knew he could not afford to get ill. The whisky still lingered – it took nothing these days – but he had needed it. Tonight would be the test, whether he had more, made it a habit again. He checked her clothes were dry and placed them on the arm of the sofa.

I can wash them later, he said, and she seemed confused. The salt, he said.

He let the dog out the back, put the kettle to boil.

A minute later he heard the girl in the hall. She was working her way along the wall, trying not to put weight on her ankle. She'd put on her trousers, but had kept his jumper on, which looked even bigger on her this morning, the arms traipsing like an unfurled straitjacket.

I'm making coffee, he said.

I need to pee.

He looked up the stairs, gave a nod but said nothing. She

huffed, sat on the bottom step and worked her way up backwards, like it was a child's game. He could carry her up, he supposed, but couldn't bring himself to offer.

Would you like some breakfast, he said, but her attention was on the stairs and their negotiation. He listened as she found the bathroom, tried to imagine what standards other people had.

The flush takes a few times, he shouted up, told himself not to fuss.

He needed to make a decision about work. The girl seemed in no hurry to leave - owing to her ankle, he supposed - or to contact anyone, and despite there being little of value in the house, he had no desire to leave a stranger alone here for any time. He would walk to the village and call the yard, say he was ill. There would be no sympathy, only a reminder that others could replace him if he made a habit of it. If the girl left soon, he'd go in this afternoon and finish late. He could use some rest himself, knew it was dangerous to keep asking of the body when it was weak.

He heard the flush finally work, the door open, the strategy of descent shifting to something more upright, a hop of sorts. He took the coffee into the lounge.

I have to call work, he said. You can stay here today. If you've nowhere to go. Until you feel better. He hadn't planned to say this, the words a surprise.

He placed the cups down and sat opposite her.

Will your wife mind? the girl said, her voice still hoarse.

He looked at the dog. It's just us, he said. If she felt threatened by the absence of someone else, she hid it well.

I always wanted a dog, she said. As a child. Our mother said they take too much looking after.

This one's no trouble.

My friend had one, but it was taken by a bear.

He looked at her nonplussed, wondered if her brain had gone too long without oxygen, or whether his own hearing had been affected by the water.

In Romania we have lots of bears, she continued. It smashed through three doors to get to the dog, carried it off to the woods. My friend heard the cries for ten minutes.

His mind formed the image, found it both gruesome and comic. He knew nothing of other countries and realised in that moment that he'd like to.

Do they ever take people? he said.

Just the tourists. If you go up in the mountains, you enter the food chain, and not at the top. They are fast, the bears, faster than people. At least if you are with someone, you only have to outrun them.

He took a moment to get it, enjoyed the humour. Felt grateful for it.

There was the silence again and he tried to think what to say. The situation was at once absurd and unsustainable. Yet here she was, in his home and not adrift in the ocean, awkward yet apparently not frightened.

It felt strange to feel accountable for something beyond himself, beyond the dog, even if only for a day. There was something natural in him that kicked in, and he thought, yes, everyone must have this capacity for kindness, but then he thought of men he'd met who hadn't. Who were built otherwise and had no such thing in them. And then he remembered that once he wasn't so different from those men.

The fire should last while I'm out, he said. I'll fetch more wood in when I'm back.

Your name, she said as he reached the door. I do not know it.

Hallam, he said.

He waited for her turn, wondered if there was any gratitude on her side for last night.

Anca, she said.

He nodded to the dog and it followed him.

H E WENT OUT through the garage and recalled the old Austin parked there, how he and Blue used to sit in it there, take turns steering or doing the gears, his brother offering sound effects that always led to a mock crash. As children their father drove them around the local lanes on Sundays. There was no destination in mind, the inherent pleasure of driving enough, he'd say. Family time. And he said that they – the road people – put passing places where it was known cars would meet, like there was this science in it. For years this spurious logic was accepted by them, their father giving a hum of approval each time cars converged by one.

See, their father said.

When they did have to reverse, their father would grumble that someone had positioned one badly, that a mistake had been made, a miscalculation. It was only in his early teens, finally seeing his father's teasing, that he learned not to trust what people said. When their father left for another woman and the exit wounds of divorce formed on their mother, it was this image that endured: the man imparting phoney wisdom from the driver's seat to his new family, his new children.

Blow-ins, the locals termed them in those first months, or *emmets*, which he later learned meant ants; you were outsiders for at least two generations, went the story. It was a superstitious land they had moved to, built on Pagan myths, on tales of treasure from wrecked galleons, Spanish bullion on the seabed. There was subterranean treasure too: tin, copper, china clay, mines and quarries now largely abandoned – wealth always dug for in those days. A fiercely independent people, always governed from afar, reluctantly ruled, heightened by the fact the county was almost an island, was its own domain save a few miles of rock joining it to the mainland in the north. And inland the bleak moor, reluctant to yield its secrets, place names you had to learn how to say, the pronunciation nothing like the spelling. This was their new home, as it had become his again in adulthood.

Outside, light fell between the dispersing cloud. He rehearsed what he'd say on the phone, knew he'd be down a morning's pay even if he left now. A family member unwell, he would say, in need of looking after, which wasn't such a big lie.

Beyond the garden, out over the cliff, a pair of fulmars rose from the sea fret and tacked into the south-westerly, the sea perhaps quarter of a mile out, feeling its way back in. As a child he'd barely appreciated the coast, beyond it being a vast playground; had no sense of the beauty freely given. Perhaps a life needed its turbulence first.

He thought how the sea always drew the eye, the swell patterns familiar, like faces, its creases and white-capping inducing a hypnosis. And he imagined it had always been this way, a thing to worship and fear and respect. That it would outlive everyone. It seemed like a madness that he was in the water last night, beneath it, how close she'd taken them to death. And yet he'd chosen to go in, there was no getting away from that.

As he walked behind the dog, he felt the heaviness in his

limbs, like he'd spent a night out on the boat, or the first few days in the cell, when sleep was something you only remembered. The thought of the fire and the chair and the whisky, this is what had kept him going in the water, the knowledge that no state was permanent.

When sleep had come last night, it was riven with images of his time inside, when all you could do was shut yourself down, like a hibernation, but one you remained primed in, like a dog resting. Each time he woke, he had checked on the girl, reconfigured the blanket, made sure her ankle was raised. She'd removed his jumper and had both arms stretched outwards, as if poised to dive off the sofa, and he wondered what her dreams looked like. He felt her head each time, tried not to wake her. By the second or third occasion, the fire had burned out and he left it, instead fetching the bedding for his chair.

He thought now how easy it would've been to have ignored her plight, mind his business. To hear a week later of a body washed ashore in a neighbouring cove, to read who she was in the paper. There was a time when he'd have felt nothing, watching her submerge and not surface, and it troubled him that this was no longer the case. Someone he'd shared a cell with once drew a bladed toothbrush up into a man's cheek and he had felt nothing at the sight. A mouth made twice its size, an ear-bound smile that exposed the back teeth and beyond. It was just an event, this laceration of flesh, like any other thing that happened in a day. You simply observed it. The grief in him, he supposed. Inured you to everything.

Yet the girl's situation, despite it being of her choosing, had given rise to something else and he had risked his life for it. Perhaps even performed something heroic. Not that she had seemed grateful. And perhaps on recovering she would simply repeat her efforts but with more success, his actions only prolonging her misery.

The dog was doing its herding, back and forth to him, the illusion of leading. He picked up the coast path, could see the phone box in the distance, the village proper, thought how the walk had seemed so much longer back then as an adolescent. The house would have been rich with the aromas of breakfast in that other time, their mother taking guests' orders, her paisley apron and cherry red lipstick still vivid in his mind. A home made alive by movement and purpose. Their father would help out too before heading to the school a town away, where he'd secured work as a supply teacher, Hallam and his brother grateful it wasn't theirs.

At its peak Seafield had five guest rooms, four of them doubles, up to a dozen people sharing the house in the high season. 6 p.m. was the usher for drinks and music, their mother playing old jazz records as she took her first gin of the day. Guests often joined her, took advantage of the generosity, and it was easy to see now the undoing of it all.

Their father had his own ritual, vacating the pub as late as he could, perhaps hatching plans for his departure even then. Returning home he would spend long hours in the cellar, where the previous owners had a workshop, though his father never seemed to produce anything, save a sense of segregation. It seemed to Hallam now a time of great illusion, a family in waiting for its storm. That it endured as long as it did was a curiosity.

A FTER MAKING THE call he went back towards the house, but instead continued along the path beyond it, to give the dog more of a run, to collect his thoughts. The owner of the yard had merely said, Tomorrow, and he knew what was meant by this. There was no recourse, no debating it: an employer who asked no questions, who cared nothing for your past, held no obligations towards you. He'd heard about the guy there before him, who'd made a fuss, threatened to report the yard to the authorities, who was persuaded not to. You forewent holidays and sick-pay, accepted safety was given scant consideration, only in that an injured worker was a useless one. Burns were treated on site, or, if severe, a day or two's absence, unpaid, tolerated. One time he removed his helmet prematurely, a weld flash from someone's gun causing mild retina burn. He had bathed his eyes in milk when he got home, but still the pain had arrived in the night, like hot sand rubbed hard into the cornea. He was a good worker, though, made few mistakes, and perhaps this bought him leeway today. Still, he would encourage the girl to go later, the world righting itself tomorrow.

The path cut inland a little, a deep gully navigated, before undulating back to the sea. A pair of rowans bent their backs to the wind with timeless effort. What sunlight there was reflected from the hulks of granite, as if heat still resided in them, drawing the eye like a lodestone. As children they would

34

come out this way, Blue, a year older, a year braver, his brother eager to test their nerves on some part of the cliff, perhaps a bird's nest others would consider inaccessible. Or he'd lead them along the beach until the tide cut them off and climbing one of the sea-worn escarpments was the only way back, little more than thrift and the occasional gorse bush to hold on to. He never refused his brother's incitements, keen to impress, to find a courage he didn't feel.

After growing up in a landlocked county, moving to the coast as a teenager, the very tail of England, was like relocating abroad. Like being on permanent holiday. Running like a backbone through the land's core was an elevated hinterland, but either side of this you were never more than a short car ride from the sea, the land tapering westward to a talon that probed the Atlantic. He had cried when their father told them of the move, his brother giving him something between a headlock and a hug. Schools and friends were swapped, but they were an age when kids mistrusted one another, their unfamiliar accents isolating them further. Blue – bullish, resilient – fared better, was prepared to fight his way into favour. But you couldn't beat everyone, and even he became a shadow during term.

In time his brother earned enough respect for them to sometimes hang about with the other kids, to be privy to talk of a newly discovered nesting site. Raiding them had become illegal a year or two earlier, a few high-profile prosecutions dissuading most. But by then Blue was fanatical, his collection – perhaps fifty eggs – transported in a padded shoebox when they moved house, relocated to a wooden container he kept hidden beneath his bed.

There was a hierarchy out on raids, his brother having

35

to prove himself, his nerve as well as his climbing ability, the others sending him up a tall beech in the fields out at Roundhill. The rarer the bird, the more sought after the egg, and they could walk miles on the rumour of a firecrest or treecreeper. But for sheer audacity, a rook's egg held kudos beyond its high incidence, their nests assembled on the highest, tapering branches, inaccessible to all but the fearless. He could hardly breathe as his brother climbed down fifty feet or more with what he thought was a rook's egg, stowing it safely in his mouth to keep both hands free. Reaching the ground, the tallest lad, knowing it was only a jackdaw's nest, slapped his brother's cheeks, bursting the egg to droves of laughter.

Later that weekend Blue had taught him how to blow eggs – to stop them rotting – making a pin-sized hole at either end, one slightly larger, then blowing gently into the smaller one until the yolk was removed.

This is why you only take cold eggs, his brother said. Ones that have been abandoned. Because you couldn't blow out an embryo, though he later learned there was a way, how you made a small hole and left the egg in an ants' nest for a few days, let them excavate it for you.

They swapped them like football cards, the eggs: two skylarks for a woodlark, a hawfinch for a couple of bullfinches. A swan's egg was always highly prized, owing to the danger in acquiring it, a pair of you needed, one to lure the mother away while the other went in. School trips to the zoo were never wasted either, an ostrich's egg taken by the most brazen of them. It didn't feel like cruelty at the time.

Having an older sibling was like witnessing your life in advance, like being a tourist in your future, and Blue's learnings went beyond ornithology. His brother taught him to skateboard, though he managed none of Blue's tricks. And to make a catapult from stuff around the house and garden. There were lessons in hardening conkers, in getting out of P.E. and cheating in exams. Blue always knew when an argument was building between their parents, knew the best excuses for being late. He understood girls, how to talk to them, something Hallam never grasped. It was like having an older, tougher version of himself, one you fought with and hated sometimes, but one you assumed would be there forever.

T HE DOG HAD something's scent now and lagged behind. He looked back at the house and for a moment was fourteen again, oblivious to the savagery of life, thinking that some glorious future awaited once the tumult of adolescence had been seen off. He recalled the family holidays here, before they moved down, their mother taking them rockpooling, exploring miniature shapeshifting worlds, microscopic life amid tendrils of seaweed, scrambling over lichened rocks agleam with quartz, the house on the cliff something that caught their eye even then.

He could see how nearer the cliff edge the property was after two more decades of erosion, waves tireless in their undermining, water channelling its way along faults in the rock, later expanding as ice, rupturing from within. And not only the sea's own impetus, but the boulders it employed as missiles, the air it compressed into the cliff below. Further along the coast were giant wire baskets bloated with pebbles, the sand dunes behind them planted with marram grass to check their drifting. In the end you could only delay it.

The house would never sell again, the subsidence irreversible. Twenty years, the structural engineer told him when he moved back here after his release from prison, perhaps a little more. They could lay grids of steel tendons over the cliff-face, calcify with concrete where possible. The cost, though, would be his alone, the local authority prepared to bolster the cliff base with boulders but little else. He'd tried to borrow against the property, but lenders could scarcely hide their mirth.

There was an offer - enough to do something with, perhaps even to buy a caravan up the coast - a firm building apartments for affluent surfers, second homes for business types, sky-stealing grotesques. They'd expanded either side of the village in the last few years and the company had a plot directly behind Seafield, quarter of a mile or so back. He hadn't understood at first, why they offered anything at all, realising later that they would raze it to the ground, this blight that affronted the vista. He'd given it serious thought, for there would be no insurance when the first bricks joined the beach, no relocation by the local authority. But the harder the company pushed, the more resistance he felt, the fight something to sustain him. Letters came every month or so, but he'd stopped opening them. It always amplified in his mind the sea's independence, how it would never be owned.

He called to the dog and this time it came, passing him, stopping to drink from one of the rivulets, and he chased it on, in case something's carcass lay upstream. Few rivers went quietly to their end, and he liked how they overshot the cliff edge here, announcing to the sea their return, water's great migratory cycle, always finding its way, returning to itself. And the waves surging in to unite with the fresh water, their advance a mathematical artillery, as was everything in nature, patterns repeating. Spits and dunes that were formed this way, the land fighting back - all of it subject to the earliest laws. You could only admire it. And yet the sea being lower than the land meant everything returned to it eventually.

The fret had cleared now and he could see out to the island, its silhouette from this angle a leviathan rising through the water, its lithe body segmented, head turning unflinchingly inland. It was all that was left of the old coast, a reminder that the sea always triumphed in this incessant struggle, millennia of resistance by the land undone, only this granite outcrop enduring. The island's stone buildings, he'd read, were erected by convicts bound for the Antipodes, men and women hived off in secret, and he tried to imagine such disparate existences.

A boat still sailed there twice a week, serving holiday lets, supplying the few residents who defied the elements and isolation year-round. They kayaked to it once, he and his brother, the promise of something rarer, a puffin's or kittiwake's egg, or the migrating birds who came south from Wales, resting a day before their African odyssey. It took all of a morning and into the afternoon to reach the island, the eye tricked as to its proximity. More than once he tried to give up, turn back, but Blue, whether through charm or menace, could convince you of most things.

The wind was their true enemy that day, an hour spent paddling just to stay in the same place, and beyond this a sandbar and riptide assailing them. When finally they hauled their canoes onto the beach, they collapsed and lay on the sand, his brother laughing like a demented thing. The plan had been to explore the coves and cliffs for puffin burrows, make a fire on the shore, paddle back with their cache before dark, but even Blue knew this was beyond them. Instead they sat on one of the piers, grey seals undulating around them like buoys, serenading each other, and there being mockery in this. An hour or so before dusk, a fisherman took pity, towed them back to the mainland after he was done baiting his baskets.

Visibility was good today and the island looked as close as ever. He pictured razorbills and guillemots returning there in spring, thinking that he should like to go there again someday. On occasion, from this vantage point, it was possible to see the flurries of a million mackerel on the incoming tide, the gulls tracking this bountiful mass.

Ahead the path cut between the still-flowering gorse and he tried to imagine the rail track that once lay here, the holidaying Victorians arriving in hordes, all parasols and frills, hedgerows psychedelic with colour. And the mile-long beach that hosted them, the coast now a place of leisure as well as trade. How he would have relished arriving by train as a boy on those family visits, relocation years away, the sea still something unfeasible, otherworldly. The four of them alighting with a hundred others from steam-hauled carriages, delirious with anticipation, dispersing to guesthouses only to later congregate on shingle and sand, impervious to biting winds that had crossed the entire Atlantic to welcome them. But they came in the Austin, which wasn't without its romance, he supposed, despite Blue picking fights with him in the back and their father blaming them both equally, the journey here seeming to take the best part of a day. They never stayed in the big guesthouse on the cliff edge, but still the clamour to the beach was made each morning, packed lunches and a cricket set, their mother content to read all day, their father occupied by the geometry of the wind-break, by what few pragmatics the day held.

And later, at bath time, their mother insisting they withdraw their foreskins to wash the sand out and avoid infection, and it being the first time he'd done this, the sheer bulbous protrusion of the thing panicking him, granular around its rim, the grains at first resistant to the soapy water. It was a comical image that now formed, he and Blue sharing a bath, purging their phalluses in unison like a sacrament, all sun-burned and wind-kissed.

And now here he was an adult, past life's midpoint, the time fallen through his fingers like water, and only a sea-bound house and an absent daughter to show for it. It confounded him how so much could amount to so little, and yet he never sought to add anything, as if his lot was decreed. A simple life, this was what he pursued for his middle years. Removed as best he could from its complexities. You met the essential needs, and in time this was enough: food, shelter, warmth – like everyone before him, everyone after. Thoughts could be walked off, or left behind in the cauldron of the yard. When loneliness encroached, which it could following weeks in his own company, he knew to take himself to the village. There had been a woman last year, a little older than him, from the pharmacy, a son and daughter, and for a while he thought something would come of it, the taking of a new family, as his father had. She hadn't pushed for anything, a month of simple company, yet still he felt the need to sever it before it bloomed. Nothing thought out, just a sense that he would disappoint them, and perhaps she sensed this too, as there was no beseeching on her behalf. He saw her around sometimes, but they never spoke. He used the pharmacy in the next town when needed. He still thought about them now and then, how for a while he'd believed it might be the answer, as if there were problems and always solutions to them. That you could replace a family with another.

He scanned the beach below, naked in the sea's absence, and harboured a fantasy that his boots might lie undamaged somewhere along the tideline and not a mile or more apart, sidling like crabs on the seabed.

Ahead the dog vanished into a seemingly impenetrable briar, in pursuit of some ghostly scent, likely returning later as feral and frayed as the day it arrived. At least this time of year there would be no ticks on the animal, their removal a task he loathed, these alien parasites whose attachment felt more malevolent than it should. He whistled with thumb and forefinger – a strident note Blue had taught him – knew this to be an effort wasted. Knew on some level he admired the dog's independence.

The sea was wind-brushed a few hundred yards out now, the light coming off it glasslike. Remembering his efforts of last night, a great fatigue gathered in him, and he headed back to the house.

T HE GIRL WAS in the kitchen when Hallam got back.
You should keep your ankle up, he said. I'll bring in
some ice.

She hobbled from one cupboard to the next, shifting cans
and jars about. Her hair had braided itself from the salt and
sand of last night, her smell nautical, like the rare times the
dog went in the sea. Her nails were mostly bitten down, a
residue of black lacquer garnishing them, and whereas carrying
her from the beach, undressing her, he'd thought her slight,
she looked strong in the kitchen's keen light. His jumper had
been replaced by her own top, her jeans once again slick on
her legs and he imagined her pain pulling them over her ankle.
He watched her move from one end of the room to the other,
remembered the feel of her skin, the warmth from the fire in it.

You must be hungry, he said, and she nodded.

He supposed food wasn't a priority for him, more something that either happened or didn't. He caught fish most
weeks, went to the village shop now and then. Purple laver
could be harvested when he wasn't carrying back driftwood.
They got pasties at the yard sometimes. As long as the dog
didn't go without. Hunger always passed once the stomach
was resigned to its calls being ignored. You never needed as
much as you thought.

I can make you something, he said. There are eggs.

He wanted to bring up the matter of her staying, so it was

44

out there and he knew one way or the other. Hope always came with this tyranny wedded to it; it was always better to not have any. He should encourage her to leave later.

I'll do an omelette, he said. And tea. Do you like tea?

Yes. But no milk, she said. It is disgusting. Why do you do that here?

He laughed a little, tried to think of a witty reply. In the end he waited for her to leave, found a bowl to break the eggs in.

Cracking the shells he wondered what happened to his brother's collection, whether it was still here somewhere, a part of the house he'd not searched properly, or whether it had been discarded after the accident. People with large collections had even gone to prison in the years after; perhaps their mother had found it, panicked and destroyed it. He would like to see those eggs again, he thought, their delicate, mottled shells, perched on a bed of sawdust. Like something unearthly.

He gave the girl the better omelette, wished there'd been something to accompany it on the plate. By the time he returned with his own, she had finished and was scrutinising the bookcase behind the sofa.

Are these good? she said. My parents' house has so many books. Romania is a land of stories. Of poems.

He realised he hadn't read in a while and wondered why such periods came and went. The books were his mother's, and he'd worked his way through many of them in the first year after returning. They had books in prison, if they wanted, and he took to long periods of immersion, subjects he cared little for, yet found a meditation in, company of sorts during days without end. He'd finish one and just start another straight off, no judgement or comparison. His mother's, though, were all fiction, which seemed to require additional concentration, and he had to work hard to penetrate some of them.

Do you read? he said, thinking he sounded like someone else.

Of course I can read.

No, I meant . . .

She pulled one out, blew a miasma of dust into the room, followed it with a pretend coughing fit.

I thought people in big houses here had cleaners, she said.

He couldn't fathom her mood, how it rose and fell. Again he pictured her underwater, wondered how much she remembered, why she hadn't referenced what had preceded it. Her top had risen an inch as she stretched to an upper shelf and he glimpsed again the birthmark on her flank.

She opened the book, read a line at random, gave out a small laugh.

Your language, she said. It is funny, no?

It is?

How you never say what you mean. There is always this . . . sub text.

She drew out the word, saying it as two. It was strange, this vitality now in her. That states could be transcended so easily. Perhaps he'd misread things, her actions last night something less definitive. A drunken swim, a game gone wrong. A cry for help, though she could not have known he would see her and intervene, and surely she had been a minute or so from death.

She swapped the book for another, opened it to a random page and read.

Ce o bucată de muncă este un om.

He shook his head, the awkwardness returning.

46

What a piece of work is a man, she said, the opening word barbed by her accent.

He was unsure what he felt, desiring the interaction to both cease and to continue, and for a moment he was the younger of them.

You don't know your own writers? she said with a half-laugh. We had to read this at school.

He felt mild irritation at this. Being made to feel inferior in his own house, after what he'd done for her. He waited for it to pass, then spoke.

Your English is good.

We get all your rubbish TV. It is how most people learn.

She slid the book back, took in the room as if for the first time.

You are a lord or something?

Lord?

This house.

He supposed it had a grandeur, even now. A stateliness, despite its decline. He knew little of its legacy before his parents acquired it, save that it had been built in the late nine-teenth century as a summer residence for a London banker of Irish origin. And that during World War II it was used as an officer's quarters, with Italian prisoners of war accom-modated in nearby fields. When he returned to the house, a week out of prison, the idea of living in it seemed absurd. Impossible to sell, its ownership was a moot point, his father the technical owner, yet there was little of value to argue over. A few hundred yards inland, it would be worth a small fortune, developers fighting like dogs over it. Instead, it had stood silent for twenty years, the sand and the salt, the damp, making it less habitable each year.

The girl moved to the window, seemingly transfixed by the pewter sea, the light ghosting across it, and he recalled his mother standing in the same spot, watching for hours the Atlantic's endless nothingness, somehow both inert and active. Something to be revered. An electric storm was amassing at the vanishing point, promising gales that would scream onto the land as the house dug in. Like living in a lighthouse, he supposed.

There was a submerged oak forest a short distance out, the tips exposed at low tide after a storm surge, seventy to eighty trees standing upright in the position they had grown six thousand years ago, the clay preserving them. And along the coast, the lichened craters of petrified tree stumps bore testament to the landscape's history. He wanted to tell her about all of this, its spectacle and narrative, but she had sat back down with an elaborate sigh, the fatigue hitting her.

He fetched her the ice and painkillers, said he was taking a shower. The next words that came from him were again unbidden, spilling out from a place he didn't understand.

If you want to stay, he said. Until you feel better.

She issued the faintest of smiles, said nothing.

Climbing the stairs he said her name to himself, liked the feel of it in his mouth. Anca. Like something to tether you in a storm.

A NEW SHIPMENT was arriving later in the week, from Latvia. Four or five girls, depending on how things went the other end. The man was to drive the van to a layby a mile or so from the port for the exchange. It was important nothing went wrong, especially after losing the Romanian. He'd tried to shift the blame but was the last to see her. And he was the one who spoke a little of her language, who went easy on her.

You couldn't watch them every minute, he wanted to say, didn't need to. He'd learned over time that doors could be left unlocked after the first month or so, a leniency afforded. You took their passport, fed and clothed them; knew how much they earned, when they were lying. Ensured the debt owed for bringing them here was never quite paid off, food and accommodation always more than they netted from a day in the fields or at the parlour. In the end they needed you.

Disorientation was crucial to the sense of helplessness, the farm and its surrounding landscape were like a thousand others in this hideous country. Their world was shrunk, like a child reliant on its parents.

The women, once here, were transported to work in windowless vans, no sense of where they were, the vehicle's doors opening onto the parlour's back entrance, or to a hillside of fields with few distinguishing features. And the harder you worked them, the less energy there was for revolt.

You clip their wings, his cousin liked to say. Stop them flying.

Of course, you gave them just enough hope. Not too much, just enough. It was a terrible situation, he would say to them, yes, nothing like they'd been promised. But it was what it was; there was no sense fighting it. It just had to be tolerated. Get your head down, he'd say, don't draw attention to yourself. Soon life will get better. It was the sort of thing a friend might say.

Do not get close to them, he was told at the start, and in time he knew this to mean emotionally. It was fine to visit them at night, take one up to his room. He never had, though, not even the Romanian, despite wanting to. Try not to see them as people, his cousin said. They are cattle. Just like at home. Livestock.

In that first month he would tell them how terrible the real world was on your own, the things that could happen, how the English treated immigrants. Occasionally one fled, as the Romanian girl had, but they always turned up, either of their own volition or they'd be spotted in some town, cold and hungry, and he'd go and find them. Almost like coming to their rescue. A parent attending to the runaway teenager. He was supposed to punish them, and gave the impression to his cousin and the others that he did. But there was penalty enough in the everyday, in the failure they felt at returning. Why add to this?

They wouldn't go to the authorities either – showing them a photo of their families with an address on the back when they arrived was enough. And if one did, they were prepared: a family business, legitimate, paperwork of sorts kept. Yes, they were migrants, but were here legally. No one was forced to stay, the other girls would say in interview; they could leave if they wanted. They volunteered details about work in the fields and not the parlour. Yes, conditions on the farm were not great, but compared to back home it was good. He knew they weren't believed, but he learned early on a thing is nothing without its proof.

Activities would be toned down for a while, until the police's attention turned elsewhere. And if it didn't, relocation provided only a minor setback. There was always another farmhouse to occupy, to start again. A nuisance, that was all. Once you learned the rules here, it wasn't so hard. Like at home, it came down to money, to power.

And yet this country baffled him at times. Just when he thought he'd fathomed it, some bizarre happening or other would play out and he'd realise how far from his homeland he was. He still couldn't believe the police here didn't carry guns and wondered how they ever caught anyone. They were usually friendly too, which unnerved him even more, like they were trying to catch you out. You were trusted more here than at home: there was no requirement to carry an ID card, and if you were stopped in your car, you just promised to take your documents in soon. Unlike home, officials were impossible to bribe here, as his cousin learned when offering a parking warden ten pounds to let him off a ticket. Fuck off and buy your wife something nice, he had said to the man, holding the note out like it was a done thing.

He had at least come to like bars, or pubs as they called them here. Except that you could no longer smoke in them, and it amazed him how so few people here did. The price of them, he supposed, for those who bought the legal ones. They should step up the cigarettes, he thought, given the mark-up.

That dogs were allowed in pubs, and given such a high status, surprised him too. Back home they were kept outside in cages, more a status symbol or to guard property, the hierarchy clear. Here they were adored like children, pampered and accommodated.

People here always said things such as: With all due respect, and it took him ages to realise it meant the opposite. Men washed their cars every Sunday. People in tower blocks were looked down on. Old ladies often had blue hair and lived alone or were dispatched to homes instead of living with family, which never happened in his country. No one here made moonshine or slaughtered their own animals, and he still didn't really know what a vegan was. It sickened him, yet here he was.

He looked out to the yard, watched for a while two of the women cleaning the van in quiet servitude. What's the point, he thought. It will be filthy again tomorrow. His cousin's son – newly arrived now he was old enough to choose where he lived – loitered near the girls, taking in this new world he'd been brought into. Incredulous of his good luck.

Food production formed the bulk of the girls' duties, especially if the parlour in town was being watched: planting, harvesting – often an outsourcing to larger gangs who were more legitimate. They were taken to a site before first light, left with the gang-master. He knew an example was made of the slower ones, the quicker workers praised, even rewarded with responsibility of their own. Divide and rule. They broke once for food, some sausage and bread, hot tea in the cold months.

Sites were varied, so the women couldn't get their bearings, or some days his cousin let them stay and work on the farm, disrupting the schedule. They were given an hour to themselves when they returned from the fields, before domestic chores filled their evenings. Cleaning, cooking, washing the cars and van.

If they behaved, they were sent back to the barn, a dozen mattresses on the ground, two or three to each one, in old sleeping bags. The one or two difficult ones, still unbroken, were kept behind, disciplined by his cousin, a belt, or a cigarette walked down the arm. They were all compliant in the end, even the Romanian until she fled. It was the only way to get through it. Little things helped – not making eye contact, being a fast worker – and he tried to teach them this, but often it was coming whatever.

For the prettier ones, there was only ever one outcome. The massage parlour was where the real money was made, up to a grand a day from each girl, half of which went to the owner, the rest handed over to his cousin. Shifts were twelve hours, six or seven days a week, a dozen men a day when it was busy, sometimes more. New girls often created an influx, once word got around, untried goods. Customers were often drunk, an hour spent in a bar after work, to build the courage. He would hang around some days, intervene with the violent ones, enjoyed giving back what they gave out to the girls. There were several types, and he got to know which was which just watching them enter the building.

He'd never paid for it himself, not even back home, felt a sort of pride in this. And yet, in another situation, he might have with the Romanian girl; there was something in her wildness that he liked. Her spirit. When she arrived, he'd made the case for her to stay in the fields. He knew this to be fanciful, the others mocking him, seeing through him. That first day she was at the parlour, he loitered all day, to the owner's annoyance, standing outside her door, hoping for a reason to enter, to show he wasn't like the others at the farm. But there had been no rough stuff initially and he hadn't understood the anger rising in him as he listened to the acts they performed on her. Finally, though, one had gone too far and he took all this anger out on him.

It was stupid to single one out, and yet he seemed unable to help himself. He would watch her at the farm, try to meet her eye, smile at her if no one else was about. Like having a favourite dog among the pack, that was all. Once, he'd given her some chocolate from their own cupboard, the fear rising in her, a knowledge of the boundary he was crossing.

It's OK, he said, as if he had permission, and she finally took it, hiding it in her clothing for later.

Another time early on he had covered for her when the man at the fields complained how she didn't work as hard as she could. He was supposed to deal with it, report it. Later, when he found her alone at the edge of the yard, he tried to convey this, hoping she understood his gesture and the risk he was taking. There was also still the hope she might stay in the fields then, but there was too much beauty there, and a week later she was sent into town. He'd given her some opiates for that first time, a few more than he was supposed to, and again weeks later when she'd asked him for more.

His cousin called down for coffee, like an order.

One day, he thought, how about you do something for me.

They all presumed him stupid, the runt who could only follow orders. Who did the stuff deemed too messy or distracting for the others. Important decisions were generally made without him, there being security in this, but also an arrogance. That his cousin and the others could run it alone. Even his cousin's son, barely here a week and still just a kid, had started getting a swagger to him.

He had his own plans, though, to use holiday lets as pop-up brothels, keep the venue mobile, clients texted at the last minute, a different place the next day. He didn't need the others, saw his future without them. Everything was changing and he'd not be left behind.

He put the kettle on and searched the cupboards for biscuits. The house was quiet today, his cousin doing the paperwork, the others checking the route for the Latvian delivery. Even the owl was silent, tethered on its bar in the corner, observing him with curiosity or disdain, he couldn't ever tell. It had arrived with a shipment last year, a gift from the Slovakians, his cousin at first bewildered, until someone told him they made better guards than the most vicious pit bull. It was seen as sophisticated, an affront to the English and their stupid dogs. Anyone foolish enough to break in while they were out would think the place empty, the creature's attack silent until it reached you. In reality he doubted this and had left it untethered one day as a test, the animal unmoving as he provoked it. They fed it rodents the feral cats left half-alive at the fringes of the yard, watched as the mice were chuntered whole down its gullet. A primal animal, he thought, eyes that burned with mistrust, survival that depended on it. He spoke to it when the others weren't around, confided in it.

He let the coffee brew, four minutes his cousin said, no more no less, before spitting in it, stirring it in. There was a solitary biscuit left, which he scoffed himself. He looked around the kitchen, thought how grand it was, how you could fit the whole of the house he'd grown up in inside it. And with this came the desire to tell his parents this, his brutal father who'd told him so often that he would come to nothing that he'd almost believed it. He wanted to show them the amounts of money he handled, more than his parents earned in decades. And he had only just started: the world had even greater plans for him.

It was strange, he thought, the places you ended up, the odd corners of foreign lands, with their strange food and customs. How you could still embed yourself, carve out a business with the same methods anywhere. The rules remained the same, as did the currency. They were business people with a product to shift.

Often they sold on the new girls to gangs in the north, if an injection of cash was needed. They'd keep one this time, to replace the Romanian. His cousin would choose, and not necessarily the youngest or the prettiest, but the one who was already near broken, defeat in her eyes, her lot accepted.

He thought of the Romanian girl, even now, despite the trouble she had caused him. He'd brought her in around a year ago, took the van halfway across Europe, getting lost several times, thinking he might just abandon it and jump on a train back to England. He imagined the local police stumbling upon the vehicle, finally removing the boxes of candles to reveal a hidden cavity in the floor, big enough for six small adults lying side by side. But coming back with nothing would test even his cousin's loyalty, so he had driven around for an hour until the road looked right again. The men waiting scowled and mocked him, and he thought how good it would be to finish them all, leave them half-dead by the roadside, and there was great power in knowing he could do this despite there being three of them. Instead he handed over the money, pretended to laugh at himself, play the fool. One by one he had ushered the girls into the van, handed them a bottle of water each, comforted them a little as he showed them the recess.

Usually the girls were sedated, especially for longer journeys, a little diazepam or ketamine to, they were told, make them more comfortable. You couldn't have one of them changing their minds at customs, getting claustrophobic. Even if the lure of a better life had convinced them to lie down in a dark hole in the floor with strangers at the start of the journey, one often panicked, setting them all off. His cousin had sound-proofed the hollow as best he could, but they'd learned you couldn't be too cautious. He always took his own chemical ballast on such trips too, enough to keep him awake, alert to whatever came his way.

He'd parked as usual in the yard of the farm when he returned that night, waited for his cousin to help shift the boxes, stuff they'd sell at the market or the boot sale. Half an hour later he'd lifted the cover from the hole in the van's floor, fear and sweat wafting up, four pairs of eyes squinting at the first light in a dozen hours. His cousin always smiled at them, preferring encouragement to force at this stage. They'd been told their presence wasn't strictly legal, at least to begin with, that they needed to be quiet on arrival.

But in time, his cousin told them, there would be all the work they could manage.

That much was true.

He helped them from the van that night, into the barn that would be their home for a few days, longer for one or two of them. He spoke softly, telling them everything was OK, hoping they understood his tone if not the language. As it turned out the Romanian girl's English was good, better than his own, he suspected, and she translated to the others what he couldn't. He led them to the barn, took them some food, showed them the toilet, which from the following day they'd be charged a pound to use.

It surprised him when his cousin chose the Romanian among those to stay. A rebel, he'd thought. Feisty. Like a prisoner-of-war, their duty to escape, to disrupt things. But he knew to say nothing, even now when he'd been proven right.

He took the coffee up to his cousin, who didn't acknowledge him. He helped himself to the cigarette packet on the table, his cousin glancing up from the laptop as if to say, Why aren't you out looking?

There'd been a sighting of the girl towards the coast, twenty miles or so away. It was probably nothing: one wretched, skinny girl looked much like another, at least to some. He was to take his cousin's son, check it out, but also use the trip to recce the endless unpeopled coves on the north coast, explore possible new routes. Customs at ports were more thorough each month, it seemed, and it was only a matter of time before their luck ran out, a major shipment interrupted. They were looking at small motor boats that could be moored somewhere quiet, taken out for a rendezvous with a larger vessel or a drop zone from a light aircraft, returning at night where the rocks allowed. If the routes worked, they would use them to bring in cocaine mostly, girls too on the boats. Like pirates, he thought. Old fashioned smugglers.

No biscuits? his cousin asked, and he shook his head before heading into town to push some weights.

THE GIRL HAD been asleep for several hours, the exhaustion of it all striking her from nowhere at times. Hallam pulled the blanket up, felt her forehead, then chopped some wood out the back, the exertion depleting what little strength had returned. He pictured the brothers at the welding yard, cursing his name, talk of replacing him part of a broader malcontent, a perpetual anger at the world. The younger one in particular simmered with loathing for him, and in the early months the prospect of violence had flanked them closely, as if they were animals establishing hierarchy, stags emboldened by the rutting season, the instinct to do harm irresistible. He could afford no such trouble, reconciled to conceding ground. And yet it was still there inside him, this potential for fury: fossilised, sealed behind long-built walls.

The yard itself occupied ground on the outskirts of the next town, forgotten land, its entrance innocuous, unannounced. Itinerants or nosy officials would first encounter the family's German Shepherd, half-starved, tethered to a chain, the slack of which could traverse enough of the lane to reach the more persistent visitor. When he worked there he knew to give the creature a wide berth, take a hidden path, despite being a fixture at the yard for almost a year now. Often the dog was muzzled, which should have comforted visitors but somehow had the opposite effect.

The yard's owner favoured a balance of legitimate work and orders that never saw the books; it paid not to ask, but you could tell which was which. He worked at the same speed regardless, preferring the label of someone less productive than a person who made mistakes. They were asked to put in long shifts some weeks, twelve- or fourteen-hour days, and he'd get home on the edge of sanity, the dog besides itself with hunger, and he'd collapse in the shower or go straight to bed. There'd be extra cash in his envelope at such times, nothing discussed. Take it or leave it.

It had been the first test since prison, of whether he needed the drink any more. To prop himself up through such physical toil, take the edges from the day and encourage a sleep of sorts. Before being inside he'd gone to work each day with the symptoms of daily indulgence, beer followed by half a bottle of spirits over an evening, sometimes more, knowing that he'd not feel human until lunch. That he functioned and held down work in those times seemed absurd now. He had the incarceration to thank for sobriety and found he now could take the occasional drink without need of continuing to oblivion. The girl's presence would perhaps be another test, the shyness in him in need of suppressing.

Those early days, on remand and then the first prison, the withdrawal had been at its fiercest, and he'd resided in a brutish purgatory, the end of which seemed like a myth, a thing he'd lost hope for. He'd howled and cowered in his own piss and vomit for a week, praying for the world to end. You could get most things in prison, but rarely alcohol. He even tried to summon his mother's god but heard only silence, loathing himself for the weakness. In the end, as was always the case, mind and body adapted to the environment they found themselves in, the craving morphing into something else, before receding entirely.

He brought the axe down a final time and headed out to the garden. It wasn't raining, but water hung in the air, heavying it, the cloud an insult to the day. The tide was low, liver-hued in the distance, obeying its lunar calling. Membranes of wrack bisected the shingle, desiccating in the wind. Beyond the stanchions of the old pier, a solitary figure stood a hundred yards out, digging for lugworm, and he could almost hear the slurp of mud as it was excavated. And beyond the figure, listing in sepulchral permanence, the wreck of an old herring boat, all paint peeled from its timber, its wheelhouse salt-eaten, hull heavily barnacled. To the west the island, little more than a snarl on the horizon, the sky above it leached of colour.

He walked across the garden to the cliff edge, its base quieted in the sea's absence, respite from the twice-daily union, and it was hard to imagine rock being undone by water, as if the land was exposed flesh, the sea a scalpel. The clan of wind turbines, so long a source of antagonism for the village, was a benign apparition to the east, the air thick with the scent of ozone. It was easy to trick the eye on such days, to render the sea two- rather than three-dimensional, its horizon a height instead of a depth, a wall of water, amassing like some invader. The corrugated coast beyond defending, as those throughout history who'd conquered it then found out.

He checked in his mind that the girl was a real thing, that she was the reason he wasn't in the hell that was the yard. Beside him the dog inspected the breeze for scent and tracked a gull as it cleaved the air a few metres out before riding an updraft. The animal had arrived a year or so ago, a scavenger he'd seen on the margins of the day, and he'd chased it away until a pity rose in him and he'd tossed it the last of his dinner one evening. He asked in the village, but no one claimed it, and so he let it stay. When the whining endured deep into the night, it occurred to him to remove its misery; he knew that he could, a spade to the back of its head, the animal knowing nothing. Instead he ushered it outside at dawn before heading to the yard, only to find it sitting by the door that evening, compliant, like something that knew its options had run out.

He couldn't recall any decision; it seemed like just another thing that happened; it seemed simpler to accept the dog's presence. He'd put some bedding down, an old blanket his mother used in winter, but the animal ignored it, preferring the hardness of the floor. Later the dog had tried to sleep on the bed and he'd cowed it down each time until the whining thinned to nothing and was replaced by a cadent snore. An easy companionship, he thought, uncomplicated. And in time, it felt like the dog had always been there.

T HE WIND WAS up now, gusting in brackish raids, and he felt some of the heaviness lift. To the north the sky had opened a little, light cascading onto the horizon where the hazed form of a container ship sat. The sea, so often made milky in appearance by effluence of the china clay workings, was leaden and bruised between its crests. This world, he thought, on its surface at least, more water than not, and there being something terrifying in this.

He wanted to cook later, to show the girl that he could. He remembered his mother's Beef Wellington, prepared whenever a guest looked like they had money, whether to solicit a large tip or repeat custom, he couldn't remember. Aromas of childhood food, the likes of which he'd not encountered since, long-cooked fare, flavours that seemed to secrete into the folds and fissures of the house.

Yes, he thought, the girl needed to regain strength, build herself up. It would be cruel telling her to leave until she was right again, and it was like he had some responsibility after saving her. And there was no sense in pushing her on the matter of last night; he'd been witness to its final act, but what business of his were the events to herald it? That there were no apparent family or friends shouldn't surprise him, for who would he call on were the roles reversed? Undoubtedly it was tough to fall on hard times in a strange country, and he imagined a lover who'd seduced her, whose promises fell away once she followed him here. Yes, that would be it. A spurning that in the absence of kin drove her from land to sea, a pain like the one visited upon his own mother. He would feed the girl, keep her company, let it come out in its own time. If she was unable to stand in the shower, he would bring her a bowl of warm water, even bathe her if needed.

He thought to learn some of her language, a phrase or two, to slip in unexpectedly, see her reaction. The library in the next town might have something, when he was next at the yard. So she wouldn't think him stupid. He played with a few of the words she had spoken earlier, liked the trill of them in his mouth, the mastication of them. Again he tried to get her age in his head: younger than his daughter, perhaps, though not by much. And she had this confidence, despite what her demons had driven her to. A playfulness with a stranger that people here, himself included, would find difficult.

Inside he found her awake. She was standing at the window and he made some comment about the weather, hated himself for its banality. He could see past her, to the cresting sea, breaking away from itself as spindrift.

Chopping wood, a thought had come to him, the idea gaining traction in his mind, expanding like a gas until it occupied his whole being. The thought that, although everyone else he ever cared about had left, she might not. It was ridiculous, delusional even, and yet hadn't his life been populated by unlikely events? Just that they had been tragic in nature. Perhaps the world had other plans for him now, the curse lifted.

How would they live? As friends? Father and daughter? Maybe she *was* alone here, her actions born from the deepest loneliness. They could console each other; the house was certainly big enough. Companions, to begin with. An unlikely colliding of lives, but then weren't they all.

She could help him start up a boat, a little business. He'd take the money from the developers after all, get a little place along the coast. Or if she had family she couldn't be apart from, they could travel there, he could learn her language, start over.

Without warning a self-loathing crept on him, scathing, mocking him for such notions. Desire and all its attendant trickery. It was the kind of thinking, the voice said, that led only to pain, to humiliation. Why would she want any part of his life? What exactly did he have to offer her? There was no money, no means to earn it legitimately yet. He knew nothing of how the real world worked; he had skills, but only practical ones. He knew about things, not people. He hardly even knew where her country was on a map.

The feathered thing in his chest now returned, absent for months, he realised. Or not absent, merely diminished, a moth instead of a bird. Flighty, restless, it could scupper any good thing, send him deeper into the house's bowels, deeper into himself, for weeks at a time.

Better that the girl went as soon as was possible, so he could get back to a routine. To fill the silence he asked her whether she had any siblings, back in Romania.

A brother, he is younger than me.

Do you miss him?

Of course I do.

She did this, made him feel less worldly than her. He already knew not to take it to heart, that it was just some cultural anomaly, an absence of empathy or reserve. He supposed

65

he liked this in her, someone prepared to contradict him, even if it meant being impolite. It was more honest: a range of responses, unfiltered. He had two emotional states: neutral and the one he'd worked to repress. In prison he had learned to turn it off, a series of beatings finally correcting the impulse. Still they had tried to coax it out of him, to see if he could be broken, and like a beast that's flogged daily, he had turned on them once. Something of Blue in him after all. A solitary riposte, to show that he could, but otherwise he yielded. In that sense, prison worked, the association made between actions and consequences, an education given by men schooled in violence, who knew little else.

Do you have brother or sister? she said.

He thought about the question, but chose not to answer, leaving her to fill the space.

There is much about my country I miss, she said. The sweet watermelons, tomatoes that taste of tomatoes. Why do yours taste of nothing? Fruit that smells so good, and pickled cabbage with smoked meat and sour cream. And your soup is so bland. You need to use all the animal.

He felt the urge to disagree, to defend his country's cuisine, realised he didn't know what this was, save the meals of childhood. He wanted her to taste his mother's food, to tell her how guests came back again and again to savour it. But mostly he was content to see this animation in her.

Why did you come here, then? he said. It sounded defensive, which he hadn't meant, and he tried to soften it. For work?

She nodded and the awkwardness between them returned, and he knew he'd said the wrong thing. He wanted to ask about the burn marks on her arm, why she hurt herself.

What had broken her heart. Instead he asked about her family.

My parents have a smallholding, she said, near Alexandria, in the south, a few hectares. They still use horse and cart, the fields ploughed by hand. We produce all our own food, salt and sugar the only things we need to buy. Clothes too, we make at home. Life happens slowly there, the old ways preserved. Scythes and hoes and sweat. My father or brother sleep out at night, to protect the sheep from wolves, and my mother milks the herd by hand, twice a day. It is very physical.

He found the image absurd, an anachronism, but not without appeal.

It is a simple life, but it is disappearing.

How come?

The young all go off to the cities now. We want more from life than our parents had. Some turn to tourism, run traditional guesthouses or riding schools, but ski resorts are becoming popular. Motorways. The forests are chopped down. You can only resist the modern world so long. Change is always coming to Romania, marching over the hills.

He wanted her to keep speaking, what he'd first regarded as a sharpness to her accent, now something he delighted in, as if she were a seasoned storyteller.

It sounds a good place to grow up.

It was difficult for my parents, before the revolution. It still is. Reform is never easy.

Will you go back?

Of course I will go back. Nothing here is like they said.

There was anger in her again and he didn't know how to make it better. They fell into the silence and for a moment he wished he was at the yard, or out on the boat.

How is your foot? he said.

She dismissed this, as if pained by the weakness, or perhaps seeing it as an ushering.

I would have been OK, she said, and after a moment he realised she meant in the water.

Outside the wind had a spite to it, like a thing of malevolence, and you could hate it on these days as it held up your progress. The sea, closer now, was brawling with itself, its momentum coming from this malice. Cloud bruised the sky, the heart of the storm no closer, perhaps destined to miss them. He looked up to the window, wondered if the girl was still cross with him, saw beneath the eaves the mulch of a swallow's nest he'd not noticed before, compacted in like mortar. Beyond this, more slates from the roof had succumbed, like missing teeth, and he made a mental note to replace them, to ward off the elements as long as possible.

It was a house built on a tapestry of sound: a dozen different winds, waves that growled and pummelled. The *rark* of gulls and the *seep seep* of their young. And underscoring this, the sea's white noise, coming without beginning or end from its machinery. Orchestral but formless.

When silence finally came, in the fragile spaces nature afforded it, it discomfited him, drew attention to his thoughts, to the things missing in a life. A wife and daughter. Where were they now? Abroad, he had last heard. Spain or Portugal. There had been cards once, from his daughter at least, formal, alluding to little. She had written to him in prison too, and he'd slept with the letter beneath his pillow for the ten months they'd had him.

The dog had joined him now, unbidden, and he thought

68

about the life it had before arriving here, the arbitrary attachments to form in life. How all things that came went in the end. Everything borrowed. He should like to hear what his daughter was doing, the things that filled her days.

Autumn, having clung on as long as it could, was lapsing now, its mellow light rinsed from the landscape a little more each day, replaced by something harsher. He tried to picture the garden in that other time, but couldn't, remembering only a couple of weather-beaten benches corroding in the spumes of brine. It was calmer on certain days, he was sure. A rare stillness, butterflies loitering in the heady scents. He'd had plans for it after returning: a vegetable plot, a new stone wall to protect it from the Atlantic's salvos. Now overrun with weeds, it served well as the dog's toilet, the far side used occasionally by fly-tippers, piles of rubbish he'd allow to accumulate until it threatened the beach below, and he would move it to the road, call the council.

When he left all that time ago, a family of his own nearing, he hadn't supposed he'd ever return, not to live, to occupy rooms his parents had, like someone from another age, drawn inexorably back by some force, as if the future was always written before it came to pass. Had he given up on finding someone? He supposed he had. And yet with each hour the girl was here, memories surfaced of the pleasantness found in the presence of another, like a warm liquid travelling to your stomach. Just knowing someone was in the next room and the pleasure in this.

Afternoon had acceded to early evening now, dusk inching down, blunting the day's hard edges. He considered all the paths a person could take, and whether those ignored still existed somewhere. The strangeness of life, he thought. Better to just regard it as a story. Something spliced together.

Inside he fed the dog, told Anca he would make some food in a while.

I can cook for us tomorrow, she said, the words to him like a hymn.

H E CLAMPED THE curve of bleached driftwood, smoothed the roughness from its edge with some coarse paper. Nothing in him was built for this, he thought, the making of something to look at instead of to use. An ornament. He considered the wood's journey, the continents it may have visited, the role such flotsam had once played in delivering new species to foreign lands. There were locals in the village who made a seasonal living with such secret alchemy, manipulating and assembling pieces into some kind of art, and he tried to recall the form of such things, the classes he'd attended in prison. Such workshops though were always rooted in the practical rather than the aesthetic. To make a table or a stool: this is what he knew, what wood was best utilised for. Perhaps he could fashion her some furniture instead.

He looked hard at the driftwood, tried to conceive what it might become. You needed an image in your mind, of the final thing, a template to work to, yet nothing came to him.

Was there not art in what he did at the yard? Fabricating steel sheets to a molten state, fusing them into one. Creating what had not before existed. He found the process not without its beauty, the coalescing of oxygen and acetylene, finely adjusting the blowpipe's flame until its feathery white cone diminished. An improper mixture of the gases and the metal would either burn or become too brittle; done correctly the pool of liquid metal became smooth and golden, like melted butter, two distinct entities cooling into one. Not merely bonded by an additional agent, but unified, becoming the same thing. And then there was that first flare as the weld-gun's flame hit the steel, an iridescent burst of brilliant white heat, violent and irrefutable. Like the forming of worlds.

If not art then perhaps a kind of old magic.

As with the traditional fishermen here, the welders too would succumb to those with greater technology: 3-D bespoke designs, laser-cut sheets, all robotically welded. The men at the yard would be forced to cut more corners, take ever greater risks, until the next accident could not be avoided. The owners would blame the workers, move onto something else, some-where else. Or perhaps they would discard the evidence, seal the person in their own steel crypt, a bespoke chamber welded shut and then buried. Maybe such a contraption already existed, in waiting, or had already been used.

Rain assaulted the small window as if thrown, the subterra-nean workshop, normally a place of benediction, now altered. Like a cell, he thought. A place to reflect on your sins, and for the first time he resented the space. Even the dog had aban-doned the room, seeking comfort upstairs with the girl. He supposed smugglers had once used the small door that opened onto the cliff face, goods hauled up, hidden in the cavity that now served as storage for his empty gas bottles. He'd forced it open once, like a portal, the sea and wind greeting him, his insignificance laid bare before him. Forty feet or so, the drop, and he recalled Blue shimmying down it early that first summer, could see even his brother had fear in him that one time. There was scant purchase, a series of narrow sills in the rock, and Blue's fingertips whitened by the weight of him.

Finally his brother leapt the last eight or so feet, pretending for a moment he'd badly injured himself, Hallam rehearsing what they'd say to their father, how they'd disobeyed him: *You are never to open that door.* The ultimate enticement; what did he expect? Blue finally stood, all sand and laugher, calling up for him to follow, that it wasn't as high as it looked, that he'd catch him, and them both knowing he shouldn't.

And for a while he thought he might, perhaps to impress, or just because he trusted his brother, a climb he had no chance of making, a broken leg or arm the best he could hope for. Yet there was merit in this, he remembered feeling, as if to say no to Blue was more harmful. Like paddling to the island. One more time, he thought. If you ask me one more time, I'll do it.

He had collected the key for Seafield from a firm of solicitors in the town that day – it had taken them an age to find it, another to verify who he was, this parvenu whose family had become the stuff of folklore. As he picked up the coast path he felt their glare on his back, the ripple of gossip spread outwards. Even the gulls seemed febrile as they flanked his progress out of the village.

His father had written to him in prison, told him he could live with them for a while, until he got himself sorted, and he had for a week. But the rules, the memories, were worse than the cell he'd called home for almost a year, and he left without explaining himself, his step-mother, he imagined, relieved, perhaps his father too. You are not my family, he recalled thinking. The terms of his licence restricted movement, but he convinced his probation officer that his rehabilitation was best served by a fresh start. Any offence could mean a recall, so stay away from trouble, the woman had said, as if he sought it, which he supposed he had that one time.

When he reached the house that dubious spring day, he saw the windows had all been crudely boarded, the ground floor ones irresistible canvases for young artists with spray cans, kids born long after the place was last inhabited. The local authority had wrapped it in warning tape, a condemned building, a fading sign on the side gate prohibiting entry. On most sides of the property, what passed as a garden encroached the windows, as if curious to witness a realm beyond itself, giant thorned tendrils forcing their way behind the boards and into rooms, eager to stake a claim before the sea did.

The front door had swollen over the years and at first he thought they'd given him the wrong key. When finally it shifted from its jamb, its progress was halted by the mound of post accumulated since their departure, a mulch of circulars he shoved aside with his boot, his mother's name on some of it, the lower levels yellowed, like strata. He listened for voices, his brother's or their mother, coming to fetch the mail, or to greet him.

After closing the door it was hard to know what to think. For so long he'd fought to remove the memory of Seafield from his mind, and in many ways he had achieved this. Certainly the details of rooms were hazed, perhaps mis-remembered. It was inconceivable that he might one day return, yet here he was.

Despite having lived there barely two years in that other time, the emotional onslaught soon gathered, as if each room possessed myriad phantoms that now rushed to welcome him, and he baulked in their presence. A place could retain energy; he could perhaps concede that. Still they came, like memories yet somehow more tangible and he ordered them away, began the practical assessment of the house.

He knew there'd be no electricity, but it seemed the water supply had also been interrupted. Several of the rooms held evidence of illicit occupation, squatters who'd entered somewhere, utilised whatever shelter and comfort could be had. As far as he could tell they had moved on, though for weeks he slept lightly, anticipating an encounter. Some of the rooms sustained the graffiti of the exterior. Otherwise it was as you'd expect a damp, unoccupied husk to be after so long, and he wondered if his ambition was foolhardy, as his mother's had been.

And yet it was his, the first thing of note he'd owned, his father happy to sign it over to him, this representation of a life the man still preferred to deny. His father had tried to sell the house several times over the years, but each survey prospective buyers conducted revealed a structure awaiting decimation. Experts disagreed on the timescale, but were mutually reproachful in the eventual outcome: nature was quarrying Seafield from beneath, and one day it would take her.

He identified four rooms as priority for surviving – his former bedroom, the kitchen, a bathroom and living room. If he could immunise these from the elements, it would allow a functioning of sorts. Water was his immediate challenge, solved in those early days by the spring that rose a hundred yards west of the house. He'd harboured ideas of diverting it, even cantilevering its supply up to the property, but the authorities would soon learn of this, and he doubted its legality. In the end they reconnected the supply at his request, and there was something miraculous in the turning of taps to produce not silence but a guttural splutter and, a few seconds later, water. As long as he occupied the house, regardless of whether he paid for it or not, there would now always be water.

Rain had slanted in over the years and rotted much of the upstairs flooring, and with no means to buy timber, he had laid down plastic sheeting, allowing a slight camber to collect the run-off and protect the rooms below. Even today there were parts of the house he'd not been in for months, perhaps longer. Like parts of your mind you never visited.

The walk-in pantry off the kitchen still had some tins of food that day, as if the squatters had no means to open them, or had worked their way through the rest, the last few not to their taste. Shelves displayed half-used cleaning products from another era, rat poison, and he remembered their mother's tears when it proved effective. Vast drapes of cobwebs clung to him as he inspected cupboards and nooks that had once been favoured hiding places. Despite its size, it still felt to him diminished, supposed to a child it was a mansion.

Beyond water and food, warmth had been the next priority, and after checking the chimney off the living room was clear, he spent two hours collecting driftwood, finally exchanging work in the village for a steady supply of logs. Those first few fires had sealed in his mind the concept of residing in the house, that however ramshackle and fugacious the structure was, it could be a home for now, and he said the word aloud, realising for the first time in his life the power in it. Home. And you were never quite alone with a fire.

It would be the small things he'd value now, he thought, those things taken for granted until they were removed. Liberty had seemed like a burden in his twenties; now it was everything. Choosing how to live, how to spend your time.

The simple act of fishing, collecting wood, lighting the fire, were undertaken more as ceremonies than errands, and there was a dignity found in them, something incarceration took from you. Days possessed a structure now, a peg you could hang your life on, and he knew he'd never be able to return to prison.

Slowly he'd reclaimed more rooms and felt a connection with his mother in doing so. With Blue. It surprised him the parts of the house he'd forgotten, domains of no concern to a teenage boy, and it was the discovery of these that gave him particular pleasure.

He released the wood from the clamp, laid it down, tried to figure out what it might be. Arranging several kindling-sized pieces coming off it, he saw it could be a bird, the arc of its wings, feathered contrails, a knuckle of a head. He would bore small holes to connect the distinct parts with twine, better still some fishing line. The eyes would be a challenge, not the cavities but what he filled them with, to give it life, essence. Sea glass perhaps, glued or wedged in. When the rain had blown itself out, he'd search for some, gather more pieces for the wings and feet. She would like a bird, he thought.

The girl was still asleep when he went upstairs, and so he walked into the village, bought some food. Later, once she woke, he made her ice the ankle for a good while, the swelling reduced now, though not yet capable of full weight-bearing. He grilled some plaice he'd bought from the quayside, cooked some potatoes. They ate together, on their laps, the silence of it amplifying the sounds their cutlery made.

He finished his too soon, watched her fork apart the flakes, wishing he'd eaten slower. She asked for some butter, and he fetched it without annoyance. It was all meat where she came from, she said, fish something you had on holiday, if at all. Her voice had a melodious quality now, as if arranged, and whenever she spoke he longed for her to continue. And when he was away from her, down in the workshop, or out walking, his thoughts were like graffiti writ large and vivid on the walls of his mind, and he could find no escape from them. He thought of the cultures in which you became responsible for someone when you saved their life, played with this concept for a while.

Later, after the food, he poured them some whisky and her face recoiled when the liquid went down, like a child's. Tiny sips, he said, but she tipped it into his and stuck with the water. He lit the fire, glad of something to do, a thing for them to focus on, as if someone else was in the room. The dog had taken to furling by the sofa, the girl able to coil its fur on a finger, smooth it, and he knew he could watch this forever. This scene, he thought, like something he'd once longed for, until it became easier to deny the longing, seal it away. He had gone to speak, to put some words to the thought, but knew it would be the whisky speaking, and so he invented some task that needed doing.

Sleep didn't come easily, and when it had he woke with a fever, a chill from being in the water, he guessed. He got up and changed the sodden sheets, the dog thinking it was time to get up, and so he let it out. In the kitchen he poured some water, looked out at the enamelled sea. Next door the girl emitted the softest of snores. He thought about the pliant parts of her, tried to imagine a coming together of their bodies, his own a disappointment to her, its years of neglect since prison. Hers this lithe and perfect thing. He thought of the age difference, enough to be conspicuous but not unheard of. His wife had been younger than him, though only a few years.

It always confused him, how lives aligned, the things that brought people together, and he wondered if a woman walking into the sea could be one of them. Certainly, her newness had wrested the house from its slumber, enthralled as it was by her presence.

Did she think him at all attractive? Would anyone these days? He should smarten himself up, take off some facial hair. He had long since grown immune to the musty odour his clothes surely secreted. Underwear was deposited on the floor of the shower from time to time, hung to dry in a vigil of sunlight, hygiene something to ward off the manacles of sickness, nothing more. Apart from his mother's room, there existed only one mirror in the house, the occasional, askance observing of it offering up a savage apparition of himself, a near-feral being, if he was honest. He allowed a beard to develop shortly after prison, a garland to negate the need for facial expression, and had grown fond of the anonymity it offered. His hair, coarse and now partly silvered throughout, could be tied back when at the yard or out on a boat, or let fall to his shoulders. He supposed there existed somewhere pictures of the other person he'd been, kempt during the years of his marriage. Wedding photographs, even.

He recalled removing the girl's wet clothes, how his feelings had shifted between paternal and lascivious, flints of a forgotten arousal sparking in his mind. It was preposterous, the prospect of it, yet wasn't his life marked by such anomalies?

The air, too, seemed charged in the spaces she vacated,

like a scent but more than that, and he would occupy them until the quickening of his blood passed, careful not to be seen as following her. He had always found relief in the places between his thoughts – the automation of himself – but since the girl's arrival such silence no longer existed. She had colonised his mind and he wondered how thoughts began, how something came from nothing; an energy, he supposed, but one you had no say in.

He should go to the yard today; no point inviting more turbulence. Though wasn't some new phase of life amassing, one where the normal state of things begged to be flouted? He owed them nothing, not even the smallest loyalty. Had he not always found a way to survive? Why not take the money from the developers, recast the dice? To have what others have. He'd always thought in terms of type, that some people had things in life and some didn't, a taxonomy. That he was someone who didn't. He had given up on happiness so long ago now, forgotten the form and shape it took, and to his surprise the thought of it evolving was unsettling. He tried to dismiss it, told himself that things cannot change in two days. Yet wasn't the world recalibrated? Each time he returned to the living room, convinced of her absence, or that she had been imagined, there she was.

He wanted so much to tell her about his brother, that day in the woods and all the aftermath, and wondered why he hadn't. If he showed her that you could lose so much and still carry on, he thought. That her compulsion for death would pass.

He went down to the workshop, scrutinised the driftwood sculpture again, mocking himself, these artistic pretensions he'd had yesterday. Imagined her laughing when he presented it to her, asking what it was, this curious creation. Trying to be something he wasn't, he realised. He lifted the bird and brought it down hard onto the bench several times, tossed it back on the pile of firewood.

T HEY SET OUT, five adolescents, across barleyed fields, tramping down pathways like arteries, idling in the heat of midsummer. The others insisting on a convoluted route, sometimes backtracking, as if leading them to a clandestine camp, and the power that came with this. They were in his brother's year, boys with an aura of menace, who could lurch from amiable to malevolent and back again in a breath. Volatile, like a gas. They swaggered, smoked like it was something they'd always done, the hierarchy unsaid yet irrefutable. He and Blue underlings, the privilege of accompanying the others granted for some as yet unknown reason. A continuation of the initiation.

He understood none of the in-jokes or catchphras-es, assumed his brother did. Violence, or a watered-down version, was ritualistic, appearing from nowhere. Punches to arms, headlocks, displays of martial arts moves that looked half-learned. And every so often these aimed at Blue, who shrugged them off like someone refusing a dance, something in him hating the holding back. Hallam was more a target of words than assaults, mockery that called into question his sexual experience, or lack of, his undeveloped body. When offered a cigarette he went to take it, his brother snatching it away, answering for him, the others laughing as Blue, to appease them, lit it himself, stifling a cough as best he could.

Soft cunts, the tall one said, the words, to Hallam, unsustainable together, like butter in a hot pan.

The others boasted of winnings from the alleyway behind the school sports hall, coins tossed to a wall, a successful trajectory coming from the wrist, as if the activity rivalled for technique sports played on the other side of the brickwork.

The day had this feel of a pilgrimage, as if a great distance was to be covered, long hours ahead of them, their destination perhaps an esoteric site few had been privileged to witness, a rare bird. He wondered about the size of the others' collections, whether they dwarfed Blue's, whether or not today would grant permission to view them.

At one point, where a quadrant of fields met, they discovered an adder looped beneath a sheet of corrugated iron, its dorsal patterning confusing the eye, as if it had no end or beginning. Just all middle. A prehistoric thing, it seemed to him, at once fascinating and unsettling, and for a moment they all stood in silence, beguiled by its strange beauty. An inert creature and yet they could sense its great kinetic energy, felt it worthy of their respect. One of them worried it with the end of a stick, and its slow movement was like liquid silk. It was both vulnerable and imperious, and whereas another animal would likely have been extinguished at their hands, the sheet of iron was merely laid back down.

Time slid by, as if at their behest, fitting around their movements, dictating nothing. Further on and the woods spiced by pines, summer a promise you could believe, school almost done. There was terror in this, he realised, his brother, after exams, moving on to another phase of life, leaving him. He knew it was important to make friends, that you couldn't be choosy.

They shifted deeper into the woods, the tall one every now and then taking his knife to bark, marking territory like a dog. Still the promise of some great treasure, a rare species, a nest site you trusted to no one. He watched Blue's gait, felt pride in its poise.

It was good to get away from the house, from the abrasion he sensed between their parents. He recalled it in their old home, a sickness hanging on the day, and had hardly noticed its absence when they moved down here, until it returned like a tumour. Perhaps this was just what marriage was, a sequence of diminishing circles of warmth. And yet there were still hollows of joy they fitted into, a moment when the four of them – mother, father, sons – remembered their roles, their lines, and it was like it had once been.

After an hour or so they arrived at the foot of a tall beech, the others pausing, announcing wordlessly that this was their destination. His brother put a hand to the tree's lustrous bark, smoothed it like a horse's mane, and they all looked up, saw that it rose to another world.

He wondered how Blue knew it wasn't just jackdaws again, after the last trickery.

There are no low branches, his brother said, meaning nothing to get purchase on, and one of them produced a rope from his pack and threw it at their feet. Blue picked it up, tested a section by snapping rigid its slack, stealing stares at the others.

Not you, one of them said, him, and fear rose in Hallam at all that height.

Told you they're chicken shit, the tall one said.

He'll take too long, Blue said, and took the rope over to the trunk.

Its length was enough to loop over the lowest branch and fall back to them, his brother fashioning a slipknot, easing it upwards until it was taut. He tested it some more, swung back and forth a foot from the ground. They could have helped, the others – offered bunk ups to give him a start – but didn't. On his third attempt, Blue found enough leverage to reach over the lowest bough and heft himself up.

If you touch him when I'm up there, his brother called out, I'll fight you all when I'm down. I'll lose but so will one of you.

And so he watched as Blue leavened through the latticed cluster of the tree's limbs, bobbing and weaving like a boxer, testing potential routes in his mind before committing. Neither was he too proud to retreat a few steps, recalibrate the course as a climber would a rock-face.

Last summer they had both scaled a smaller sycamore, his brother lifting him up the more challenging sections. There had been no nest, but they stayed aloft in its core for an hour or so, watching the world from the hammock of a crook they'd each found. It was the safest he'd felt in life, unseen, both part of this world and yet not, his protector a few branches above.

Blue was high enough now that the rooks got some sense of his presence, a mammal-like volume rising from morsels of chatter into bursts of serrated chiding. Wing-beats starting up in applause, alarm caws issued like spitting fat.

By the time his brother was parallel to the first nests, the sky had darkened to a formless mass, bird morphing with bird, chaos and order. Still he progressed, edging out along one of the tapering boughs, hands and feet like an efficient piston. Blue had told him his theory once, inherited from the badlands of home, a calculation to test the weight-bearing property of a branch. Once you could touch forefingers and thumbs around it, you went no further. That's why rooks build their nests there, his brother had said. A compromise. Exposed to the elements and predation from the air, but nothing without wings gets to them.

Except Blue, Hallam thought.

He tried to calculate the height of his brother: forty feet, perhaps more. Twice as high as he'd ever been himself in a tree. Impossibly high. The rooks mobbing him now, this strange new predator inching itself into their colony, shredding the air around his brother in furious sorties, a rhapsody of shrieks, strident and demented. This innate, mechanical response of all things, he thought, to protect their young. An ancient calling, diminishing your own worth for the sake of the species.

And still his brother there, holding his head tight to the branch, unable to risk freeing an arm in defence, waiting for a pause in the onslaught that wouldn't come. One or two rooks venturing close enough to jab and claw at flesh. The boys beside him on the ground, now grinning, entertained by the spectacle they had engineered. And himself, unable to find breath or to blink, both horrified and enthralled at Blue's exploits, this gesture undertaken in his stead.

On and on, the birds kept at him, their programming knowing only this. And his brother docile now, the torque in him gone, but still calculating the odds, still thinking it possible. Six feet from the nearest nest, a few more shuffles through this storm of birds, what seemed now like the entire rookery coming at him, the attack a thing of synchronicity and wonder. One egg, he thought. He is only going to take one egg, and he almost spoke it. Beside him, the others had quietened, even they in thrall of his brother's bravado, perhaps even scared of it. The noise everything now, barbed and colliding with itself, no beginning or end to it, the sound of life resisting death.

When the branch cracked it registered as an intrusion, a catalyst to something else. The rooks, too, seemed to sense it, easing their intensity a little, perhaps knowing that a shift had occurred. And the second crack, louder yet ushering in a near silence as bird and branch and brother began their dispersal.

A shower of everything from this spectacle now falling to them, nests and tree and Blue, rooks treading air above this and the silence thickening. Every now and then a protruding branch toyed with his brother, altered his shape and course. The thing happening both slowly and fast.

Blue hit the ground a dozen or so feet from them, an unnatural sound, of two things coming together that shouldn't, his shoulder folding in on itself, a brief flail of limbs, head claiming its own patch of ground to collapse into. A crumpling, and in that moment all humans' failed attempts to fly, as a vapour seemed to leave his brother.

And then a stillness, save twigs and leaves confetti-ing him, birds alighting onto branches, laying fresh claim to the tree, those with nests intact returning to them, the others ponderous then indifferent. A dozen or so broken eggs garlanded the ground around his brother, embryonic forms emerging from shells, featherless and translucent, some with small movements. Flight never known, only plummet.

And his brother, this indomitable warrior, now unmoving and silent, the air between them thick with an awfulness, and it seemed absurd that this had happened. This shifting of one world into another, and him witness to this juncture, to birds dead and dying, all their evolution undone, his brother somewhere between these states. Waves of nausea now, almost separate from him, a pulsing of their own, and his knowing there was both something he should be doing and nothing that could be done. The birds overhead beginning to quieten, and inside his chest something feathered too, flighty and panicked, immobilising him.

He sensed the others running, as if in trouble and that putting distance between them and this site was an effective tactic, and for a second he thought to do the same, to flee what had built all day and had concluded in a few seconds. To be no part of it or of what would follow.

Then some instinct forcing him towards his brother, this abomination of rearranged bones, misshapen yet intact, like something thrown there. Something in need of fixing. A coil of blood made its way from Blue's ear along the dust of the ground, probing the terrain for least resistance, sometimes halting and pooling, then altering direction a little, gathering specks of the earth in its flow. The ground between them like half-dry cement as he made his slow way to Blue, as if to witness his brother close up was to condemn him.

He spoke his name, invited him to get up, remarked that it was some fall, that he would boast of it for ever. He placed a hand on his brother's back, felt the warmth in him. Tried to ignore limbs that disobeyed their confines.

He wanted to recall the direction they'd come, figured they'd walked a couple of hours in total. The sun would be a clue, had they lived here longer, bearings taken, Blue leading them home like some expert tracker. If he walked an hour, there would be something to recognise, the gully they'd ran through, a couple of coast-bound seagulls, perhaps the adder. He couldn't rely on the others fetching someone. There was nothing to do here. Whatever needed doing was not here.

And yet there was no moving in him, this the only place that existed. He sat down against the tree and heard himself humming a tune their mother taught them as children.

HE PICTURED HIS brother in those months after, stricken within himself, how it wasn't right to keep someone like that: you would finish it off, were it an animal. Allow the thing its dignity. The law, though, was clear: there was enough life to preserve, a carcass that with nutrients administered could continue a functioning of sorts. And of the early days of wires and tubes and hope alternating with despair, his parents drinking from lunchtime now, though never together, more unsaid than said from now on.

He had stroked his brother's head by the tree, told him it would be alright, and finally – after a minute, an hour, he didn't know – he ran. Retracing as best he could the outbound journey, thinking on some level if he moved across the land quickly enough that time could be reversed. Every now and then he fell, grazing palms and knees, the pain a wanted distraction. Finally he recognised the topography, knew Seafield to be just a couple of fields away. He ran into the house, the breath needed to speak all gone from him, his mother casting a look of disapproval at the tears to his jeans. There was this great temptation to go to his room, to take the knowledge of this thing with him, deny its assembly with reality. Surely if he just went to sleep the world would recalibrate itself.

It must have been three hours before Blue got to the hospital. His pelvis was shattered, left arm and leg broken, none of which would be treated until he was stable and could be sedated. In the meantime, a coma was induced, the bleed on his brain their focus. A man came out of the theatre, talked them through it. How the scalp would be sliced and peeled back like hide, a section of the skull cut away to relieve pressure. He found comedy in this, that they would glue the piece back at a later date, like a broken vase. The scalp then drawn back over, secured to itself again, brain separated from air and light only by skin. Where would they keep this piece of his brother's skull, he kept thinking. What would happen if they lost it?

Four hours later and they were allowed to see Blue, watch the ventilator rise and fall, his brother this fleshly thing kept alive by pumps and wires.

They visited twice a day to begin with, frequency diminishing as progress did. At first he saw his parents pray for the removal of danger, pledge to accept anything in return for this. Let him just survive, they urged, unknowing or uncaring of what this could mean. Then came terminology that captured none of Blue: statistics, coma scores.

When he came back to them, it was as another species, unspeaking, unmoving, alive as a plant is alive yet without growth. They spoke to him in vigil, their mother drawing with her knuckles soft circles on his cheek. At home they talked around the matter, never about it. Hallam was never asked for details, only how high Blue had been, how long he'd taken to get help.

A progress of sorts occurred, glacial, barely noticed. Everything would have to be learned anew, they said, reconnect muscles with their signals. Some small speech returned, more a noise than words, a refrain of anguish. Finally, there came a transition off the acute ward, returning for operations when he was able. His brother began to feed himself clumsily, like an infant in learning, more an indulgence than anything as he missed his mouth again and again. The realisation specialist care would forever be required, that Blue would always be something tended to, even as an adult.

And then the lexicon at home shifting, his brother airbrushed a little from each day.

You're an only-child now, his mother had said one evening as she watched from her window the sea squalling in, and he turned the phrase over in his head for days, knew it in time to be both true and false. Knew the absence would grow and grow, that his brother would become folkloric, life defined as either pre- or post- that day, not just for Blue, for all of them. Forever an approximation of himself, the boy who hadn't cheated death but merely borrowed something from it.

He wondered what his brother knew in those two years after the fall, a mind consigned to – to what? The thoughts of a child? Or worse, of mental processes that were lucid and mature, yet beyond expression. Communication reduced to a primitive exchange, a pre-language where words – often just a sequence of profanities – took minutes to form, brief windows sanctioned when fatigue and despondency receded. Movement coming vicariously, limbs lifted to be washed, torso turned like a pig on a spit.

Weekly visits to a common room occurred, where his brother would be lowered into a window-side chair, head supported by a horseshoe cushion. Spoon-fed and another form of protest as he spat food over a tireless nurse. Comatose patients, he supposed, at least had insentience going for them. It seemed unfathomably cruel that Blue should have lived every one of the days to have passed since that day in the woods.

During one of his final visits, he had watched as his brother stared vacantly into the mid-distance, perhaps registering a pigeon scull by, climbing in his mind one of the tall conifers across the lawn. Did he remember the fall? They said he probably didn't, that his anchoring memory of his former life was likely moored somewhere earlier that day. A dream sequence, repeating, forever inconclusive. And his own replaying of Blue's descent, looping ceaselessly in those first months, the silence of it, the un-noise of the fall, something beyond comprehension.

He read to his brother from magazines, told him about school, about kids ghillying for crabs off the sea wall, as the two of them once had. He spoke of their home on the cliff as if it were a person, with its own memories and sadness, thought of its empty rooms, like his brother, using only a small part of itself.

And later, when it was just the two of them, a silent plea issued from Blue's eyes, to do the right thing, and he wanted to give this finality to him, but all he could do was hold his brother's hand and squeeze it.

THE WATER'S COLD was like some ancient thing, like it had always been part of her, part of everything, and Anca felt this connection to everyone to have known it. A childhood memory amassed, of her parents taking them to the coast and seeing the ocean for the first time not in a book or a painting, and the awe of it, its unknowableness. She'd read about the sea gods of other cultures, the lore of her own landlocked country rarely in need of any. Of real-life giants that dwelt in its depths, clandestine and noble. She tried to imagine the first person to cross a vast terrain to meet this non-land, to witness its spectacle, its ebb and flow, and in that moment their desire to traverse it, to connect with other people. To locate the rim of the world and watch the sea fall from it. And realising this person had no way of knowing they were the first, the moment lost on them.

The ferocity when she'd entered the water had for a moment overwritten her mortal impulse, the body's instinct to survive almost beyond her will. She knew the English phrase *come to your senses*, and supposed it meant this, an obeying of the corporeal despite your intent. Like putting your hand in a flame, you couldn't urge it to stay there for long. And yet each wave she negotiated, the more accepting her body became, the sea's clench becoming a conspirator, a force to work with, not against. Initially, the current too tried in bursts, delivering her back to shore – a maternal gesture perhaps, warning against itself. As if issuing a test, for her to show that her efforts were earnest before it permitted entry.

Yet she surged onward, the water level rising imperceptibly around her, its gentle wrestling of her a reminder of its vastness, and there being solace in this, the interconnectedness of all the oceans, the insignificance of herself.

Somewhere beyond the discomfort was a fiercer throb where she'd fallen the last section of cliff, her ankle turning on landing, but she was soon able to consider it something separate to her, the cold, the weight-bearing water, in her favour. Physical unease was something she'd learned to tolerate in the last year; there was a box you could place it in, next to the one for emotional pain. It was how you survived, a learning she'd made early on at the farm. The less you observed pain, the more you undermined it.

She sensed her breathing start to return from its panicked state, felt more in control again, this thing she had chosen to do, a reclamation. See it through, her mantra.

And yet.

For the first time her feet could no longer touch the seabed, her body now given over fully to the ocean's whims and desires. Her clothes now a second skin, tugging her downwards until the bottom was reached again and she had to hold her breath. She half-swam, half-pogoed further out until there was nothing for her feet to find without her head breaking beneath the surface.

She tried to gauge the rhythm of the waves in the gloaming, sense their frequency so she could close her mouth before they were upon her. It was just as easy to hear than see them, a soft churring, barely anything. Up wave and down wave she was taken, and she found some strange pleasure in this, despite it all, the more she gave herself to the sea, the more accepting of her it became, as if the test had been passed, entry bestowed. She tried reaching down, to remove the ballast that was her shoes, but the coiling of her body took her under each time, fatigue elongating her until she gave up.

A half attempt to swim before pausing to recover, letting herself gently rise and fall, treading the water with small steps despite the pain in her ankle. A gull cried out from the gloom, hardly any distance away, mocking and spectral, its own realm adjacent to hers yet sovereign, intangible.

She felt the sea as a living thing now, a conscious entity, and she was happy to give herself over to its womanly wisdom. It was everything land was not, an untameable netherworld, and she thought of the first water to exist, wondered if these were the same molecules, whether it worked like that.

She needed to go further out, to make sure of it – no point doing half a job, of making a gesture. More misery would only come from this.

Turning to see how far the shore was, the direction of things was lost for a moment, almost all of the day's light now gone as the sky charred. There was an island she'd observed the last few evenings, hazed on the horizon, and she imagined being washed up on it in a day or two, one further removal from this place he'd led her to.

Where was he now, this man whose name was probably a lie also? How many more like her had there been? As appalling as it was, there had been small comfort in wishing she wasn't the only one, that others could be as naïve.

She hardly thought of him these days, the hatred and sorrow mostly spent. Unhappy, though: she at least wished he was that.

Finally she saw the old house on the cliff, its silhouette on the coast path, a glow leaking from one of the seaward windows. She'd assumed it abandoned – there had been no lights the previous evenings, at least from the aspects she could see, many of its windows boarded up. Its configuration reminded her of the farm, the barn that had been home for the best part of a year. How even that squalid place had become a sanctuary of sorts after they'd taken her to the parlour in the town.

She could recall none of their faces, the men who arrived to take brief ownership of her: their features had morphed into an apparition, a medley of mouths and noses and eyes that her mind rendered nebulous. Something to be grateful for perhaps, that her final images would not be of those who lay on her, excavated her, and she tried instead to conjure her parents' faces, her brother's, who she supposed thought her dead.

She would always smell the men, though, the foulness of their cologne and sweat, the alcohol and tobacco on their breath, enduring at a deeper level in the memory, easily retrieved despite the layers of scents laid over them. Even now, with the brine and nautical air profusely upon her, it was never far away, their stench.

The woman in charge at the parlour had told her there were rules, things the men were not allowed to do, unless she wanted the extra money. It was up to her, and the autonomy surprised her. The man who drove her from the farm made no reference to this, only that she should do as she was told, that it was a temporary thing, the best way to pay off what she owed. Take yourself somewhere else, he had said, and she'd been confused until she realised he meant in her mind.

I don't know how to give massage, she had said to him on that first day before they arrived.

Just do like the other girls do, the man said, his eyes losing some of their harshness and she'd understood then. Massage did not mean massage.

He'd driven up close to the door, a rear entrance, and took her in. It'll go quicker if you're busy, he said, a thread of concern running through his voice. The first one is hardest, he said, and she wondered what he knew of such matters. Even then she thought how unlike the other men at the farm he was, and her instinct was borne out when, unseen, he began passing her confectionary a month or so after her arrival, something they never got. Pieces of chocolate in foil, a biscuit, the inference being that she didn't show the other girls. He must want something, her first thought, that it was in exchange for something down the line. But it never was – the men at the farm could take what they wanted anyway, with or without walking a cigarette down your arm. And when she did escape, the suspicion that he might have been looking the other way, that some part of him hoped she'd get out.

That first day, before they went into the parlour, he'd handed her a small plastic bottle, shaking the contents to illustrate what they were. These will help, he said, just one or you'll fall asleep, and she remembered the groggy feeling the pills had given her on the journey over. He'd indicated for her to take one and so she did.

Those febrile hours in the floor of the van, lying like canned sardines next to the other women, drifting back and forth, perpetually nauseous, sweating then shivering, certain she would die. The first real sense of there being a terrible mistake, of a great foolishness.

It will be uncomfortable, they had told her with all their charm; just focus on how good life will be at the other end.

The girl next to her sobbed the whole time, and Anca held her hand, finding comfort for herself in this. They'd been told to keep quiet, were given masks for the fumes. A coffin, it seemed, packed tight with strangers, dark and squalid. And there was no way she could know the worst was to come.

INSIDE THE PARLOUR that first day, the woman in charge had shown her the room she'd work in, the bathroom they all shared to get clean in between men, a kitchen where they could make drinks. There was a waiting area where you were allowed to talk to the others, though few of them spoke her language, the ones who did content to make small talk but little else in those first days. Later, when she had been accepted as one of them, they furnished her with the wisdom of survival, how to treat the soreness, prevent infection. How to cover up bruises, which men never liked to see. To sense when a man was getting angry. In return she taught them the English she knew.

At the start she was the only one from the farm, the others preferred for the fields, stronger than her, she presumed. They'd made her pick fruit for a week, long, physical days and she'd wished to be anywhere else, thinking if she was slow she could stay at the farm instead. And then one morning, queuing to get in the van, the man ushered her into the house, told her to undress and to turn around as another man looked on, gave a nod of approval, and she realised it was nothing to do with strength, who got to go to the fields.

Her clothes were not suitable, the woman in charge said that first day, and there was a chest of drawers with stuff to try on for size, a cardboard box to keep her own things in until the end of the day. She chose a turquoise bra and pants, shoes that elevated her and took practice to walk in. Conscious of her birthmark, she learned to stand obliquely, her better side forward.

That first time the others eyed her up and down without apology, and she remembered thinking this was something she expected from the men, the women perhaps keen to assess the competition. They were, to some extent, rivals, she supposed.

How long have you been here? she asked one of the others, but the girl had merely smiled unconvincingly.

An hour passed before that first occasion, a period of time that seemed to swell and contract as she occupied it, and it was peculiar, that all the paths of her life had led here, and she thought of all the escape routes she must have missed. Men came and went in that hour, sometimes not even looking their way, instead heading straight out the back, whereupon one of the girls would finish her cigarette and follow. Thirty minutes later it was usually over – an hour if they paid more, she learned – and she thought at this point that it was perhaps something she could endure, if it was only for a while and not that often. She was not a virgin – there'd been the boy at summer camp, and the tall gypsy who'd so betrayed her. Neither had been pleasurable, the act fretful, rushed, but in the parlour that day she was grateful for these occasions. Perhaps this was just how it was, a brief and painful union. Think of it as a mechanical thing, she told herself. *Take yourself somewhere else.*

When the man was shown from the reception to where the girls waited, she knew he would choose her. This sense that if not his first time, then it being early on in such behaviour, that they had this in common. Around forty-something, slightly overweight, he tried at first to not make eye contact with any of them, issuing a hand gesture to suggest any of them would suffice. The woman again encouraged him away from such reticence, told him to take his time selecting. His gaze swept across them more discerningly this time, his confidence rising a little, and with each sweep he settled on her a little longer. She tried to look undesirable, hunched her body a little, pursed her lips to make them thinner until she felt the glare of the woman in charge. Either smile or look seductive, they had been told, though she found both difficult on command. Look at all these beautiful women, she urged him silently, you cannot want me. There was fear when finally he did point to her, but also resignation: the moment could not be postponed indefinitely, and the man was perhaps not as grotesque as the previous ones. It may as well be you, she thought.

She wondered about all the names there were for what she was about to become, felt strangely accepting of it. She repeated the driver's words in her head: just get the first one over with. Willed the tablet to kick in more. She took the man's hand, as they were told to do, and led him to the room.

She'd almost entered the water last night, a stubborn vestige of will instead returning her to the village, to the garden shed she'd found open that first evening. There were berries in the hedgerows nearby, and a man had given her some change as she sat on a bench near a row of shops. She filled a large plastic bottle she'd found in a waste bin with water from the public toilets. It amazed her how much food people threw away, a circuit of the village offering up sustenance to rival that which they were given at the farm, though none of it warm. You could live like this for a while, she told herself. Things usually got better if you waited long enough.

In the daytime she wandered around the village, trying not to attract attention, all the while hoping someone would take pity. But she realised she was a ghost to the people here; they saw her from the corners of eyes, but chose not to look, and she wondered how they knew what she had become, as if she exuded an aura of squalor. She thought of her own country, the custom of welcoming visitors, taking them into your home, sharing whatever you had with them. It was shameful to do anything less.

But it seemed no such tradition resided here.

Whatever she had thought escape from the farm looked like, its reality came quickly to her on those cold nights in the shed. She had no documents, no right to be in the country. What she did at the parlour was surely illegal, the authorities would put her in prison, or worse: return her to the farm that wasn't really a farm, where no animals grazed, no crops were produced. She had no money, no friends, no family. It was what the kind one had said, that she was better off with them despite everything.

THE CURRENT SWEPT her up a little, dropped her back down. He came to her mind now, the man she'd met back home, who'd blazed into her world from nowhere, blown her heart wide open. He'd given her a cigarette after the dance, offered to walk her back, something she'd normally decline. But there had been more arguing with her parents earlier that evening, the lure of prolonging her return enticing, and so she'd accompanied the tall, charismatic gypsy, content to listen to him talk in the moonlight.

He hoped to attend the next dance, but asked if she would see him again before then, and so they'd met the following week and shared some țuică he'd brought along, her head made incautious and dreamy by the sweet alcohol, her chest warm and prickling. The air was spiced and heady, a symphony of crickets everywhere, nowhere. They walked for miles, along a woodcutter's path and up into the hills, every now and then pausing and she was certain he would kiss her, though he never did that day. She remembered thinking there was an age gap, that her parents would be angry at this, but reminded herself she was almost eighteen, that decisions in life were becoming more and more her own. She didn't want the life they'd had, the back-breaking toil, a life so simple as to be crushingly mundane. The world was about to open itself up, a host of glorious possibilities. And the man with the big brown eyes and way with words, despite being from the countryside too, knew about the city, how it had transformed since the revolution, modernised. He spoke of the opportunities there, of fashion and art and ambition. She was, she supposed, mesmerised.

They had been seeing each other for a few weeks, when he mentioned the UK. How much work there was, what you could earn. Enough to send some back to her family, to buy things they never had.

Your English is good, he said. They want people with two languages.

She could work in a big hotel, meet famous people. They could rent a big house, she could go to university, become whatever she wanted. She could travel, immerse herself in new cultures. It all happened so quickly. She would go there first, he said, a friend already had work for her. He needed to sort out his passport, and would join her as soon as he could. They had to choose quickly, he said. Before someone else took it. It was the maddest thing she had heard of.

She hadn't said goodbye to her parents, her brother. They wouldn't allow her to move to Bucharest with a gypsy, let alone abroad. Frivolous people, her father would say, who made no provision for winter, who came begging when their own supplies had gone. No, it was better not to tell them and have a scene. She would explain it all in a letter; they would see it was a good thing once money arrived.

The gypsy man had taken her to a part of the country she hardly knew, introduced her to men who would take her on the journey, quiet men, men whose eyes alone took something from you, but by then it felt too late, a thing with its own momentum now. A small apartment and more girls arriving, though not from Romania, the men passing cigarettes, eyeing them without shame. This is just a temporary thing, she told herself.

Five of them in a truck, for hours, offering each other half-smiles. When they finally did stop, she thought they had arrived, congratulated herself. But it was only to transfer into another vehicle, this one smaller and she couldn't work out how they would all get in it, the man who would later give her chocolate showing them this hole in the floor. They were given a sip of something strong, a pill to take, told to lie down tightly together. He handed them a bottle of water each to cling to in the darkness, told them to make it last.

In the past year she had counted all the moments she must have known and wondered why in the end she went so compliantly.

I will join you very soon, the gypsy had said to her, and she repeated the words until she had passed out.

The sea was part of her now, as if trying to connect with the fluid inside her, to break her down. She was exhausted by the effort to expel the salty water each time a wave broke on her, her weight dunking her below the surface. Swimming was no longer an option, so she lay on her back, wishing that the moonlight of the previous nights was upon her. Anca pictured the other girls in the barn, their varied routes across Europe to the same pitiless destination, a dozen stories all different yet the same. How in the cold months they huddled up at night, the act unspoken, a primal response to survive, like animals. Like the cattle back home.

The strangeness of curling into a woman, she thought, and this being too much for some of them. There seemed no judgement, though, either from those who could not bring themselves to, or from the men who roused them at dawn to go to the fields, as if they'd seen it before, and she supposed they had. When she first arrived one of the women had shown her a conch shell in the far corner of the barn, how you could place it to your ear and hear the sea.

She drew on these oddly intimate moments when at the parlour, when the flesh on hers revolted her, imagining instead the tenderness that came from stillness, this connection with someone who would not harm you. Nothing sexualised, more a kind of solace, a silent comradery. Her days so brutal, the nights a balm and wishing them longer.

The man that first time had been nervous, and she had to reassure him.

What would you like, she said, and he said he didn't know.

There was this oddness from it being both something she was choosing to do and yet it being against her will. Some terrain between the two. The pill she'd taken had given soft edges to everything, like the *ţuică* but warmer, like she was being held, and she was grateful for it.

They sat on the bed like this for a while, like embarrassed teenagers, until he pointed at her bra, so she removed it. Took her pants off then too. And all his shyness went.

This time she didn't resist the water as it took her down, the breath holding itself on instinct. That would be the start of the end, she supposed – a breath. For now she could still swim up if she chose to – go further out, even change her mind – yet no such desire to leave this icy womb came. She opened her eyes to the pregnant blackness, sensed the granular texture of salt on them, a few blinks to accustom them to it. She let the current twist and snag her. Further down and there was a ringing in her ears now, something building, like a pressure. Finally, her body breathed for her, in spite of her, the urge to choke intense but brief as water flooded her lungs, the panic like a fire sweeping through her, chest burning despite the cold sea now inside. Air a few feet away and its possibility became everything, the only thing, and she made some strokes with arms and legs, hoping up was up.

A mistake, then, in thinking she could, in thinking that she wanted to do this, and in that moment there was no past or future, air now everything. Terror in not even being able to try to breathe, her body in stasis. Frenzied kicking now and the sensation of pain in her ankle, and trying to focus on this pain instead of her lungs, pain being a wonderful thing now, an alive thing. Then her arms grasping hungrily for non-water, and a few seconds later their movement easier, the sea's resistance gone, her head lurching through the surface and choking like she was something turned inside out. Somehow lying on her back, head to the side, lungs exhuming themselves, water forced out to where it belonged. Her ears clearing one at a time, sound entering her like life starting up, and she heaved and wretched, felt the first of the air reach inside her, the sea breeze on her face the most beautiful thing ever. If she had the strength to laugh, she would do so, at this birthing, at the realisation she wanted to live after all. Then a wave arced on to her, bigger than any before, and she fought to stay afloat, realised how enfeebled she was, the choice something she had given up, the fight gone from her. More kicking and flailing, like a fit, and for a moment she thought this could be turned around, that the sea would deliver her back to shore, where she'd limp to the shed and life would somehow start again.

But air again became water, and there being no effort left to summon, sound skewing and gurgling in her ears, and she held her breath in, tried to make a prisoner of it as she sank. An outbreath bringing a moment's relief but with it the immediate compulsion to inhale, as irresistible as water itself, and hoping the end would be quick, consciousness lost in a heartbeat rather than dwelling, coming and going. The inside of her waterlogged again, the terror lessened a little this time by knowing the sensation, body primed for this unfamiliar state. Nearly two decades of breathing halted. How had she thought she could do this? All the other ways it could be done. Then thoughts themselves requiring too much exertion. She felt herself to be in a kind of motionlessness, unbreathing, unthinking, unmoving except the gentle descent, like a leaf in air. Everything falls, she managed to think. Bird and fish and mammal. The blackness of before now absolute, all parts of her cleansed of those men.

S HE WASN'T CHOSEN often in those first weeks, something the men sensed in her perhaps, her timidity, her inexperience. But as the terror in her receded, replaced by resignation, she became as popular as the others, perhaps more so being the youngest, and there became a curious conflict between them, as if the women's rejection of her, even amid such horror, was an affront.

After that first time she expected it to always be rough, the grabbing, the pounding, the pinning down, so it surprised her when men weren't. Often they were gentle, considerate even, a different kind of dread rising in her at this. Sometimes they couldn't finish and bowed their heads in embarrassment, and she would comfort them, tell them it was OK, that it was still amazing, the best ever, and sometimes they believed her. Other times they'd blame her for the absence of a climax, salvage some pride this way, as if a breach of contract had occurred. Some fell in love with her and were politely 'offered' one of the other girls, or on occasion excluded from the parlour when they asked to meet her elsewhere. Some wanted to kiss her, which seemed more intrusive, more intimate, until it happened and then it wasn't intimate at all. Somehow it was easier to detach emotionally from a penis inside her than a tongue, and she wondered why this was.

She hated the sounds her own body made, resented its moistness, the act of treachery in this. They were given lubrication should they need it, but she never did.

Some of the men were cruel and she learned how to sense this beforehand, wondered how much this was reserved for her, or whether their wives and girlfriends were also subject to it. Perhaps this was her worth, to soak it up so the other women in their lives didn't have to.

Men's preferences were varied and unpredictable. Some liked to lead, others to be led, and she pretended she was an actress auditioning for a part. Some insisted on obscure positions, odd angles that put great strain on her back and joints and took strength she didn't know she had to maintain. She was coerced into various roles, from submissive to aggressor, entire scripts she had to stick to, phrases to repeat, crescendoing to their vocal climax.

Some requested the absence of a condom, a thing you never agreed to. One of the other girls had shown her how to put one on a man, a courgette serving this particular purpose, a brief moment of hilarity touching the day. Even the non-violent ones tended towards a furious rhythm near the end, anger in their movements, hatred of themselves for attendance, or at her as the instrument of their deviancy, she wasn't sure. It was like they were trying to leave all their hate, their sins, inside her, like a bee leaving its stinger, and she wondered how much of this could fit in one person.

Some liked to pull her hair, arcing her up from the bed, and she thought her back would break. She recalled a doll from childhood, how you could make its limbs achieve such implausible geometry, and she wondered why it had been made this way, legs that folded up almost to the ears.

One man wanted her to piss on him and so she had,

standing astride him and soaking his grinning face, and there being the illusion of power in this, although recalling it later she had vomited. Another insisted he place two fingers down her throat as he entered her from behind, getting off on her retching while he came.

She asked the man for more pills after that time.

In the early days she often cried, which some of them liked, were aroused by. After finishing, if there was time left, some men liked to talk, as if she'd shifted from whore to confidante, the session both hedonistic and confessional, and she imagined herself a priest, sponging all the guilt from them, as if their acts had been committed on someone else. They spoke to her like friends might, equals, as if what had passed before was the most trivial and reasonable of transactions.

She often sensed the man who drove her here, the one not like the others, waiting around outside, despite there being no need to, the parlour having its own enforcers in close range. He would pretend there was some business to sort with the owner, but she learned in time that his concern was with her welfare. And sure enough, the first one who took it too far, who wouldn't stop with the pinching and the biting, despite what she said, brought the man into the room at her cries. There was some beating in the hall and she never saw that customer again.

One day in the first week she refused, assuming they'd take her back to the fields, but another man came for her, returned her to the farm and a beating of her own. The cigarette on her arm. Later she was sent to other locations, brothels masquerading as saunas, some barely hiding the fact. The realisation that it could be forever, or a version of forever. That her debt would never be paid. There would be thousands more men, one after the other, fucking and beating her, until the relief of an age older than this one rendered her undesirable.

There was perhaps a semblance of consciousness remaining. A flicker deep in the mind, the self barely aware of it, yet something nonetheless, the thing that distinguished you from another. Barely even thought, more a dream, a passing from one state to another. A powering down. A system quietened, starved of its fuel, yet not quite ready to go.

The final trace of her, of a life. Sea all around and in her now. Glimmers of childhood and all its prismed colours. Light in the darkness, the promise of it. Entry and exit via the womb. The water not even felt as water now, no distinction made between her and it. Body and water as one, only this final spark of her lingering, an energy not quite extinguished, almost raging at the prospect of its expiry. Time suspended, like being snagged on something, yet any moment now ready to catch the current and unspool again, and there being no spark then. This thing she had determined to do, almost done.

And somewhere within these morsels of awareness, the sensation of physical contact, the only sense still in use. The seabed perhaps. Or some passing creature. Then the contact more permanent than expected. As if it were some part of herself. Or if not herself then something otherworldly, heavenly. A hand and then an arm holding her. Pulling her. Up and up.

THE VAN SLICKED through mud by the gate before finding the traction of the lane. A pig of a day, he had heard the English call it, and in the year and a half he'd lived here, most of the days had been pigs. There was a time last January when he thought the sun would never return, the low sky an endless grey nothing. It once rained for sixteen days in a row – he counted them – and all the money they were making seemed of no consolation. But finally the land awoke, the sky opened and he could make a case for it being as good as home, T-shirted days, drinking and eating outside, the girls less miserable. A couple of weeks in spring, it lasted, a collective madness gripping the entire population.

His cousin warned him summer might not arrive, and it hadn't, just long months of rumour and promise, and then after a brief flourish, it was winter again. How did people stay here for a lifetime, he wondered. Waiting for something that might not even come. Six more months, he'd give it, time to build the stash in his room some more, enough money to go on his own, start something else back home. Something in the city perhaps – he was not built for rural dwelling, not in eastern Europe and certainly not here. His own little empire it would be, more drugs than people – he was liking less and less the notion of enslaving someone. The family name would be enough to get a foothold, the old contacts telling him who was running things, who he needed to get to.

Perhaps the occasional brothel, but nothing static. Pop-ups, they were calling them here. Rent a place for a few days, move on, a holiday home. It was foolish to use the same premises over and over. You may as well hoist a flag. The women would be there by choice, if he did this, the split of takings fairer.

And then he would move more into legitimate pursuits, a bar, a casino. Get smarter with the money. You could still make as much, without risking prison. He imagined doing time here, had heard it was easier, but still something to be avoided. He'd been lucky so far, why push it?

His cousin's son lit a joint, took a long toke, then passed it to him and he felt its long reach after a couple of deep inhalations. Seventeen the boy was, still wet behind the ears – another phrase he had learned. He was to toughen the kid up in the next few weeks, introduce him more to the enforcement side of the business. Including the drive there today, it would only take a couple of hours. And then they could head to the coast, check out the coves and look for the girl.

Four days she had been missing, longer than any previous absconder. If she'd gone to the police, there would be a visit soon, unannounced, but they'd sanitised the place in anticipation of this, expanded their few legitimate undertakings. His cousin had spoken to the other girls, reminded them of the script and the consequences of straying from it. More likely she was in some ditch, and to remove this image from his mind he took more long drags.

Good stuff, he said to the boy. Better than at home.

It's alright, the boy said, making out he'd had superior, that he knew a lot.

Don't get so wasted, he said, that you're no use today.

The boy laughed, then after a while spoke again. They say

you're the one to ask about pills.

He handed the smoke back, ignored him, the van bloated with this fug. After a silence the boy spoke again.

And the girls, he said, we can do what we want?

He imagined the boy entering the barn, like a child in a sweet shop, homing in on one of them, another the next night, or maybe the same night, all the frustration of his adolescence over-spilling until the farm became just an extension of the parlour.

Just leave them, he said. They work better when they're left alone.

He could feel the boy's irritation, that this contradicted what his father had perhaps promised him. He was going to tell him that he could use the parlour, like any other paying customer, but wanted to change the subject.

Tell me about English girls, the boy said.

He laughed it off, realised he didn't know any. They seemed confident, he supposed, though it was hard to generalise. There was this huge class divide here that there wasn't at home, and it fascinated him. Like separate nationalities.

He asked the boy where he was from, even though he knew, but it was the boy's turn to ignore him, and they settled into the silence for a while.

Today's excursion only carried risk if they were being watched, and then followed. He drove around the back lanes a while, made sure they were alone. That was another thing: you couldn't get anywhere in a hurry over here, especially in this arse-end of the country, with its tiny roads that chicaned endlessly, nothing ever straight, and when you met something, a standoff occurred until the other car retreated to a passing place. Worse still you'd spend the journey behind a tractor. Not that anywhere was far. Never more than two dozen miles from the coast, a guy in the pub had told him, wherever you were. Like an island really.

His thoughts kept returning to the girl, how he'd watched her escape that day, thinking he'd pick her up an hour or so later, how he'd got high instead. It confused him, this willing her to freedom but knowing he couldn't allow it. Like one of the feral cats playing with a mouse. He'd driven around like a mad thing for two hours, every little lane, stopping at gateways to look across fields, at one point shouting her name. Later he stared hard into his cousin's eyes, watched the conflict rise in him, his cousin wanting to lash out but uncertain these days of the response.

Find her, was all he said in the end, and it being a challenge, not to see if he could, but if he would.

Perhaps she had secured work in a brothel a few towns away, he thought. It was what she knew now; there'd be no other way to survive. Word would get back if this was the case. But for now they were to head out to the coast after lunch, follow up the possible sighting. A girl with an accent, drifting like snow.

The rain came harder than the wipers could manage. The boy had his feet on the dash, portraying a bluster he knew was false, and he was tempted to hit the brakes hard, undo the bravado. It was good not to be the new one here anymore, the butt of jokes, recipient of the shittiest jobs. It meant they numbered seven now, his cousin still top of the tree, though he sensed others were circling, like wolves, a weakness smelled. You needed a matriarch, he had realised, so the business ran as a family, and despite shipping a son over once the boy had finished school, his cousin could only ever command partial authority on his own. The other four, couples termed family, though not in the blood sense, would make a move soon. Perhaps he should get himself a woman, manoeuvre his way to further power here, try to forget the weather.

They drove for an hour without much conversation, the boy alternating radio stations, skinning up once more, the weed potent, working its way to the extremes of him. He wondered what his cousin had told the boy before arriving, probably the same as the girls were promised: a land of opportunity, a chance to improve your English, a good income, which for the boy at least would be true. An apprenticeship like no other. It was hoped the boy would be good with numbers – to take care of the accounts, or better still a computer coder who could learn to skim bank cards at ATMs, help them diversify – but they'd seen no sign of an education, and so he would start like everyone else, a foot soldier.

Despite his age the boy was well developed, the kind of physique that got attention on entering a room. From farming stock, he guessed, his cousin's family servants of the land back home, generations who worked harder than he ever would, yet with nothing to show for it. All that muscle and power wasted. And the boy would only grow into himself more, hence today's blooding, to give him a taste for it. Better to show him what they did than tell him. His cousin had pulled him aside this morning, though, let him know who he'd blame if any trouble came the boy's way today.

The road opened up a little and he pushed the van harder, the rain easing now. The town emerged as a series of new-builds, which ran into more traditional properties, houses, shops, estate agents. The boy was taking it all in, the quaintness of the place, as if they couldn't possibly have any business here.

It's everywhere, he said to the boy. Every town, city. The same needs. Just better hidden here. He could see a sense of wonder beyond the boy's bemusement, the same feeling he'd got when he arrived, that life would be easy now. A good living made, with little chance of being caught. He'd watched those who came to the parlour, mostly middle-class men, or if not then monied all the same, their lives otherwise respectable, worth protecting. Same with their product, although prescription drugs were threatening this now, something they needed to expand into more. A seedy underbelly, unseen by anyone who didn't know what to look for. Nail-bars, car washes, fruit pickers – so many of them slaves, trussed by fear, knowing only to do as they were told.

Even in this place he could sense it, what lay beneath. Brothels were never publicly advertised in this country yet were everywhere once you knew who to ask, once you knew the code.

He turned the van onto the High Street now. He sensed the gazes of passers-by, tried to drive as inconspicuously as possible. Glancing down at his phone, he obeyed the grey line that wove back and forth, half a mile or so to go. Perhaps the girl was even here, and he fantasized about glimpsing her.

The man they were visiting this morning had been a conduit between them and a Polish gang a few counties to the east. He set up exchanges of girls for them, sometimes pills, sometimes powder. It was said he had contacts everywhere, with home-grown gangs, Asians, even with Russians in the capital. His own background was unclear, save that he was a native Brit, a veteran of numerous turf wars, now freelance.

They'd been introduced to him a few months ago, when they began bringing in more girls than was prudent to keep. A contact from his cousin's early days here set up a meeting. Before then, their activities here were chaotic, naïve: benefit scams, pickpocketing, shoplifting. All high risk for low reward. It wasn't until his cousin's friend came over that they began to emerge from petty crime to something more organised.

As they expanded their operations, it was important not to step on any toes, to move into territory you were not welcome or equipped to defend. And so this man, for a price, could tell you if you were encroaching onto other gangs' terrain, facilitate an introduction if necessary. Meet demand with supply.

But they learned on the last deal the man had sent their way that he'd skimmed more than a little for himself, had assumed them all wet behind the ears. Several grand, the difference between what the other party paid and what they were given, even after his take. It almost didn't matter, the amounts involved. But you had to make an example, restore your status. It was all you had in the end, your reputation.

☙

It was getting near lunchtime and violence always made him hungry. He pulled the van into the next pub, guessed the boy would benefit from a drink with his food, to put some colour back in his cheeks. It had been easier than expected, the guy on his own out the back of the shop he ran as cover. Had there been more of them he wouldn't have let the boy wade in alone. In the end he had to pull him off, a talent for it, it seemed.

You alright, he asked the boy.

The boy nodded, not surprised by what happened, but still shocked. Shocked at himself.

It gets easier, he laughed. First one always freaks you out. You did well.

The boy shrugged it off, tried to keep up the pretence.

He locked the van and they walked across the car park. They would scout some of the coves this afternoon, find a few suitable spots to bring goods in. A whole industry it had been once, his cousin had told him. The coast of an entire county used to avoid customs, contraband brought up through tunnels, hidden in basements. No doubt it was harder these days, but sometimes the old ways were the best.

He was hardly bothered about the girl now, as if there had been enough spectacle to the day. She'd be far away, he hoped. He could say they looked.

Wash the blood off your hands, he said to the boy, pointing to where the toilet was. I'll get us beer. And pasties. You know what they are?

※

IT WAS AFTER Blue's fall that he learned the true reason for their relocation, how the house was supposed to have been more than just a fresh start. That it was also to dismantle their father's temptation. A woman at work he'd found impossible to give up, even after their mother's first attempt to diminish herself with pills that retched up her insides for two days, a stomach virus they were told at the time.

They sold up soon after her recovery, exchanging mid-terrace comfort for a crumbling guesthouse that battled daily the Atlantic's barrage; their mother's logic, Hallam supposed, to give their father so much to do that there was room for little else. And for a long time it must have seemed to her the move would be their salvation, as she discovered a talent for hosting, perhaps born of the security distance from the other woman brought. She sourced local ingredients where possible, handled promotion. Despite their restricted budget she insisted on fine crockery, expensive sheets in the rooms, exquisite lace doilies for the milk jugs. Even if behind the scenes it was a more shambolic, even shabby affair, guests, she swore, would be doted on.

Meanwhile their father, prior to starting his supply teaching, renovated the least dilapidated rooms with help from an uncle, who travelled down at weekends. Locals, for the most part, thought them foolish – the latest in a succession of abortive owners – but a few wished them well nonetheless.

As boys navigating adolescence, half a country away was a vast, unfathomable distance. It may as well have been abroad, and as an adult he pondered the absence of any consultation by their parents. An adventure, their mother kept calling it. And they could always return if it didn't work out. If their father mourned the loss of his former life and its illicit dalliance, he hid it well, at least at the outset.

Six months later the guesthouse opened one sweltering Easter with just two guest rooms complete. But as bookings became dependable, there were two more by mid-summer, the final two ready the following season. There was contentment, or at least the illusion of it, their past life receding like a smoky dream.

Their mother seemed to thrive living by the sea, the saline air, the great fluid landscape at their door awakening some abiding affinity within her. With the exception of an infrequent pilgrimage to the coast as a child, and later their own trips here as a family, her whole life had been spent landlocked, albeit only a couple of hours from either coast. But their new shoreline residence was like a homecoming for her. The sea spoke to his mother conspiratorially, offered up its own sorrow as solace. It knew of mistresses, was one itself to those it lured like playthings – mariners, buccaneers, anglers. I will never abandon you, he imagined it saying to her.

His mother never met their father's lover – confrontation wasn't her way – and so the woman must have taken on an impossible beauty, the imagination cruel in its portraiture. It would have been impossible not to compare herself with this ideal, seeing only flaws and shortcomings in her mirror image. In the weeks after their father left, between her wailing and crumpling, his mother made attempts at recasting herself:

lipstick and kohl overdone, clothes that should have bestowed in her a certain glamour, sexiness even, but that somehow served only to bring the anguish into sordid relief. Her hair colour changed, the flecks of grey vanished by counterfeit hues.

Picturing her now, he supposed there had still been beauty there, that men in the village would have been drawn to in time. He recalled when he finally met his father's new woman how plain she had seemed, and he wanted to announce the injustice of it all, take his father to one side and question his dubious judgement. Surely such a departure emanated only for the most luring of beauty, irresistible and total.

Hallam understood now how his mother's preoccupation with the sea, her epic observing of it, was more than just wistful or melancholic. It was a silent communication, a paean to this faithful province that receded almost beyond sight, but that always turned and pulsed back in, frothing at its vanguard, eager to find her.

Cycles of seven, she said waves came in, the seventh the most powerful, and although he now knew this to be apocryphal, like all folktales there was probably a truth in it. It's never the same, she once said, like a child witnessing a thing of splendour, how the wind and light conspired to ensure this, each individual wave a new event. Some nights, when the moon was large and low, the glitter path it made on the water reached from the horizon to the house, and their mother stood at the window in awe of this shimmering spectacle.

He too had found himself under the sea's spell since returning, fascinated by how it ordered itself, how water bound together, uprearing into waves that spumed at their zenith. Over and over. This energy within it, waves outliving the wind that produced them, a momentum of their own now. Their angles and geometry, chaotic yet ordered. It spoke to him, the sea, in this new life he had, as it had to her, altered the internal rhythms of him. It was as far from prison as a person could get, this place from which all life had come.

But such beauty in the natural world held little sway with their father. Blue's fall, in his eye, undid everything, as if his commitment, his sacrificing the other woman, had been in exchange for a fulfilling family life. He hadn't signed up for catastrophe, for grief. This changed things.

Perhaps their father wanted her to find the letters – certainly they could have been better hidden – as it gave him the confrontation he needed. A steady correspondence over a year or more, options kept alive, an escape lane for when the brakes succumbed. Absence had only galvanised their union. He recalled their mother quoting sections of the letters from this other woman, at one point spitting words out like poison, and Hallam sensed her small thrill in the anger after weeks of numbing grief.

All guests were cancelled after Blue's accident, the house beset with silence until he went to bed, and the artillery of a failed marriage started up, and he cried for his brother to be there. It was months before their mother could face hosting again.

Later that week he returned from school to find her plundering a bottle of gin, his father's note festooning the table, a great energy coming from it. He was sorry, it said, his feelings for the other woman of a different order to what he felt for them. Seeing Blue like that had made him realise how fleeting life was, that it had been a mistake to come here. Hallam could join him if he wished. There would be money once he found work. Perhaps it is for the best, the words suggested.

He comforted his mother, said things he didn't believe. Hoped her faith would catch her. But all she said in those days that followed was: It's just the two of us now, and he realised he was the man of the house, despite being a boy.

His mother took on the air of a widow overnight, the gait of a person who would never trust love again, never invite it in. She took up smoking again, something she'd given up before Blue was born, holding French cigarettes between the very tips of her fingers like an actress, dragging hard on them as if to make up for the years of abstention. She began sending him to get gin in the village when she couldn't bear to leave the house, the man in the shop happy to serve him for such a valued customer, despite his being underage. Twice he called the doctor out for her when the binges ceased having space between them and he thought she might be dead.

Try not to leave her alone, the man had said without meeting Hallam's eyes.

And the gin, for a few brief hours, drew out some radiance from her, albeit a false light, one incapable of illuminating a house too capacious and damning for so few people. Her bedroom lamp, he noticed if he got up at night, was never switched off, and he would tiptoe up to her door, listen for the scratch of a pen or the turn of a page, but there was only ever silence.

Looking back it was clear theirs was not a family that would endure, and he tried to think of things that did, and that if land and buildings and families didn't, then perhaps there was nothing.

More letters came from their father, both to him and his

mother, and at first he demonstrated loyalty by not opening his, keeping them in a cache beneath a loose floorboard in his bedroom. He was never to mention the man again in her presence, she said. An uncle came to stay from Scotland, cousins he half-remembered flanking as a child, now at university, his visit one of duty and awkwardness.

And then it was just the two of them again.

When he did open the letters – four or five – they read as confessionals, the wording frantic at times, as if pleading for something he knew was beyond concession. There was anger there, too, at their mother's relocating them, at God for allowing that branch to break. He had to leave, he said, as if it were something forced on him.

Never did he refer to them, beyond the declaration that money was scarce and that he hoped to send some soon. Each time there was an invite to visit, to meet his new 'brother' and 'sister'. And despite his hatred for this coward of a man, he had been tempted, especially as his mother was falling deeper into despair, the house an echo chamber of grief. A fully-formed family: did it matter if it wasn't his?

HE CAME HOME from school that day, the house empty, its final guests of the week departed after breakfast. The radio was on, operatic cacophonies violating even the farthest rooms. He turned it off, the silence absolute except the sea's far off percussion, even the house's creaking and groaning quieted.

The bottle of gin lay empty on the kitchen table, and he tried to recall its morning level. The calendar offered no visitors for several days, and he realised he now preferred it when they had guests, the day more content when it possessed structure and purpose, his mother moving efficiently from task to task. Her appearance, too, varied greatly, with bookings resulting in a little pampering: a favourite dress in the evenings, tentative steps back into the world. Life went on, he assumed was her silent mantra. He helped where he could, an hour's homework before serving food and washing plates, while his mother played host, sharing cigarettes and port with those too polite to decline.

They had planned to see Blue that evening, get the last bus home, as they had, the two of them, for a few months. If his brother processed the absence of their father on such visits, it merely formed part of his silent archive, the detail logged deep in the brain's circuitry.

Does he dream, their mother had once asked a care-giver. It was hard to say, but they suspected he did. There was comfort for her in this, he realised. That the confines of a stricken body could be escaped from, Blue's nocturnal world restricted only by the totality of his memories, his imagination, a realm with more voltage than his waking one.

He sat in the kitchen that day after school, watching the sky sink, the shape of the coast lost to dusk, only the filament of cresting waves visible. He turned some lights on and looked in the fridge for something to cook them. He did this more often now; gave his mother a break when it was just them, the meals, he realised years later, bland or overly rich, though she never said so. If he was quick, they'd make the half-six bus, get a couple of hours by Blue's bedside.

It was four days before his mother was found, a couple walking their dog on the coast path, a shape that drew their attention in the cove below. Her turquoise swimming costume a beacon in the sand. A stain on the day.

In the absence of a note, the verdict was misadventure, her swimwear suggestive of a tragedy begot from leisure, as if the family were cursed and calamity in the natural world had long been their fate. She had taken to swimming after Blue's accident, and he'd watch her propel herself through the swell, graceless yet at one with the curling waves as they made a mockery of her attempts to swim, her attempts to make an alliance with it. She'd wade out, let the undertow take her, thrash through the smaller breakers, a thing in the wrong element yet determined to assimilate, to return to its natural state. The human body more water than not, and this primal desire to be adrift in amniotic waters, the origin of all life, driving her on, the sea's buoyancy thwarting gravity.

On calmer days a technique of sorts took her in fraught manoeuvres, tacking one way then the other, then floating on her back like a corpse until her energy returned. From his bedroom window, he would watch as she hauled herself back to land, reluctant to return, the world unaltered. Sometimes she'd forget a towel and he'd walk along to the path, handing her one as she stood shivering, blanched of colour, and he would lead the way back to the house, light the fire and make a hot drink, listening for the sobbing to resume.

Perhaps her intention that day had been merely to swim as normal, or that once out of her depth, looking back at the house and all it stood for, it had seemed easier just to keep going into the sea's gaping maw, letting the water enter her lungs, life and death converging with each wave navigated.

Four days the sea had his mother for that final swim, a time when she was still just missing. A toy to manipulate, to toss and plunder, and he tried to imagine her watery journey, his mother revolving in a cavalier dance, drawn down by currents before her buoyancy lifted her, her form breaking through the ocean's skin. Then plunging again, out beyond the continental shelf, deeper and deeper, where light did not penetrate, the vast tonnage of water above her, the sky a tarpaulin keeping her submerged. Still her arms gesticulating in the turbulence, windmilling her as if choreographed. And then the dance slowing, softening, as the sea lost interest and she became just part of it, an osmosis, adrift in its folds, finally something in its element, gill-less yet congruent. When, on the fourth day, it gave her up, his mother joined the wrack line almost two miles west of Seafield, curiosity for the sand-hoppers, the wading birds, the sum of her life leading here. In the end, even the ocean rejected her.

Her body, the policewoman said, would need identifying, that they would contact his father. There was no need, he said, for he was adult enough himself, which is what he felt the previous few months had achieved, though of course they had not. His father returned in the days that followed. A week later he went back to live with his new family, where Hallam would stay for several years.

The officers took him to the mortuary that day, two of them, flanking him like buttresses in waiting, but whatever part of him was needed to collapse had shut down, as if his brother's fall, his father's leaving, had shown him how life was to be, how it would always play out in a minor key.

The viewing room was cool but not cold. He had not expected the soft furnishing, the carpet, and had braced himself for a wall of metallic drawers that slid out, as films had taught him it would be. The others waited at the room's fringes, told him to take as long as he needed.

His mother was laid out on a singular table in the centre of the room, a white sheet covering her from the neck down, and he thought how peaceful she was, in the deepest of sleeps. There was something wrong with only seeing her head and he asked if the sheet could be turned down and they consulted each other, confusion about whether this could or should be done. One of them nodded and the woman came across the room and obliged. Immediately there was this regret in him, a barrier breached, his mother's nakedness, even in death, a taboo, and he couldn't recall the last time he'd seen her breasts, glimpsing them perhaps across a landing, or on the beach. He was grateful the sheet still covered her below the waist, and he shifted it a little merely to reveal one of her arms, feeling an energy and fear in the room behind him.

His mother's hands were wrinkled, like she'd been in the bath too long, her torso's skin bloodless. Her form appeared enlarged, as if swollen, and the woman explained how her own gases had done this, had built up inside her. Again the breasts like beacons, drawing the eye, yet nothing like those he'd seen in the magazine Blue had shown him that time.

Wounds where the rocks had bitten into her were bleached, waxen in appearance, more cavities than injuries. Like something bled-out, the only colour found in the blueness of her lips. He asked about the small fissures in her ears and nose, realising in the silence that she had been food for fish and crabs for half a week. Nobody in that room wanted to tell him this. Years later he would learn that had her desiccating body been on the beach longer, the carrion birds would have got to work on her eyes, on the soft parts of his mother. The circle of life.

Words spilled from the adults behind him, how the father should be present, that the identification could have waited a day longer, once they'd managed to contact him.

He asked if it was OK to touch her, taking her hand in his, knowing it would be cold, but still the chill of her violated him, all the sea's silent depths in her. He tried to rotate the wedding ring that she still wore, but it had become embedded in its distended finger. He wanted to detach it from her, there being importance in this. For years he wondered how they removed the thing, what had happened to it. Despite everything there was still an energy to her in that room; even in death her expression spoke of something that had been wronged, and he hated his father as much as was possible.

He pictured his mother, as he would in a hundred dreams after that day, ghosting across the seabed, catching on barnacled substrate, settling in a fronded cavity until the current loosened her. He knew it would have been her wish to stay there, beyond all tempests, to not be deposited ashore, back to a world that served her poorly. Better that all the discrete elements of her dwindle to watery nothingness. The skin first, flensing so that her hands resembled a pair of latex gloves. The rest following: a translucent pelt in tow behind her, shedding until it snagged on a reef and became its own being, a weightless figment of a woman shimmering in the current while her skinless body continued onward.

More likely the epidermis would break away in smaller sections, tissues of jellyfish floating into the blackness. The feet adrift next, dispersing like satellites escaping their orbit, tramping across the seabed in their own silent jive. Then the crustaceans and cephalopods would get to work, opening up the body to smaller scavengers, who would enter the nutrient-rich core of her. Finally, stripped bare, her bones would rest amid a forest of kelp, entomb themselves in silt on the ocean floor, breaking down over years, decades, an efficient and total degradation. The sea devouring her, like a lover.

Instead she washed up like any other flotsam.

They ushered him away that day, placed the sheet back over his mother, this person he'd once been literally a part of. He wondered what molecules, if any, of his mother remained in the house, in undusted corners, deep between carpet fibres, petrified by the years. He had no time for ghosts, knew only the corporeal survived before breaking down then clustering as something else. Yet even he could sometimes hear her voice in the wind, spy her head undulating far out on the up- and down-slopes of waves. His mother simply no longer a creature of the land. A mermaid perhaps.

They cremated her a week later, from ice to fire. His father, already a stranger, by his side, thin platitudes forming at the

man's mouth. A grief of sorts in his face. The new woman
– the stepmother in waiting – had driven him down, was
decorous enough to be absent. There had been talk of Blue
attending, the practicalities in the end proving too great, and
so he had described the day to his brother, wondering how
many of the words got through.

He imagined his father and the woman raiding Seafield,
redistributing his mother's possessions, keeping what suited
them. He was never offered mementos of his own. There was
a conversation about all the books, the new woman suggesting
they be left for now.

And then it was done, the law saying he must live with
his father, and there being some relief in this despite all his
hatred for the man. The decision made for him, and the house
that he would one day return to, for now relieved of them all.

H E WAS HOT. A moist heat, instead of the dry furnace of the yard. He acknowledged its comfort, despite an urge to resist it – like being in a too-hot bath. His dream was fuzzed as a result, hints of delirium, all soft at its edges, and pulses of the past days intruded, like shockwaves: the water, the weight of the girl, the dog barking. And ever present, his brother, not as an image but an energy, a sensation, like an invisible gas, clinging to other aspects of the dream. I want you to leave me alone, he thought. And I don't want you to.

The tug of reality now and his holding on to the dream, content to witness the mosaic of narratives as if from afar, cossetted by this warmth, like a containment – a sleeping bag, yes that was what it felt like.

The images faded, all colour and clarity bled from them, the presence of his room came into focus in a frail light that he supposed was dawn rather than dusk. The urge to move was thwarted again and this time discomfort triumphed and his body protested at its confinement. He tried to fathom it.

The girl held him tighter and pressed herself into the back of him, as if expecting his remonstration to take greater form, like she was holding on to a raft in high seas. Instead he was like something frozen, his muscles primed yet inert, breath shallow, barely anything at all. She was dressed, he sensed, at least most of her, and he scanned in his mind his own body, found a t-shirt and pants. He had once slept naked – in his youth, in the early days of his marriage – and he remembered its liberation.

He checked that he wasn't still dreaming. Her arm felt almost without weight, like a wren or a piece of fabric, yet it lay over him with extraordinary power, making a vice against the bed. If he wasn't dreaming then perhaps it was an hallucination. A madness. Years spent living alone, at the fringes of a community; he would not be the first recluse to succumb. And if this was illusory, perhaps the last few days had been also, conjured by an isolated mind, creating what it craved. He had thought her into being. A girl his daughter's age, periled as his mother had been, both in mood and method. And this time he rescued her; a second chance for his younger self. How could it have been scripted better?

Again, though, he knew that suspicions of insanity usually signalled its absence. A prison psychologist had told him that the last time he believed his mind was losing its grip. It was just the grief having its way, the woman had said, how it had been lying dormant, waiting to manifest. If you think you're insane, she had said, you probably aren't.

Not mad then.

As if to confirm this he checked the girl's pressure against him as best he could without moving. How long had she been there? He recalled the previous night, how there had been an ease between them for the first time and how he had thought that perhaps she could stay in the house a while longer, even once her foot mended. They had talked without the awkwardness of the first two days, and when he sensed she was getting tired, he brought her some water and turned in. He loaded the fire, said goodnight – an already familiar ritual – and a flicker of family life was rekindled, its long absence voluble.

As with the two previous nights the dog remained with her, fellow itinerants, he supposed, and he tried not to resent the disloyalty.

He had entered sleep – not as he tended to, all belligerent and tethered to the past – but with a new rhythm, a simple easing from one state to another. Is this how other people fall asleep, he wondered before finally succumbing.

The bedding was more on him than her and he tried making tiny adjustments to correct this. Any second now she will wake, he thought, and there will be a scene. She'd say that she must have been sleepwalking, that she was still delirious from the sea, that it was a terrible mistake. Or worse, she would shout and blame him, the gap in their ages made unhealthy and lurid. His account would be disbelieved, he would return to prison, all for saving someone's life. He had taken advantage, it would be said, perhaps even of her unconscious state. An immigrant, young and vulnerable, lured to the house and preyed upon. He should have let her drown.

But for now, only silence.

He tried to relax into it, but the strangeness struck him anew every few moments, like a forgotten smell, and he wanted only to prolong it, to delay the embarrassment.

His thoughts kept returning to the yard, yet he was able to repel them, the girl's presence acting as a sedative. Perhaps he should try to sleep some more, though he knew this to be impossible. Another thought overlay this one: that he could move his fingers a few inches and they would touch hers, undetected, perhaps reaching into her dreams. An entwinement. There had been several kinds of contact between them since the water, but this would be different. Different even to her arm across him, as if his reciprocation removed what innocence remained. That she had initiated their nearness seemed in no way to allow such a gesture and he remained still.

Daylight bled into the room with more vigour now. He tried to trace the latticework in the wallpaper his father had hung, as if it were a maze to be escaped from, but his mind was shrewd to such attempts at distraction.

He strained to hear her breathing, wanted to gauge something from its tempo, held his own in the silence. And then an awful thought, that she had slipped away after entering his bed, that the sea had taken her after all, its lure irresistible even on land, that her systems had shut down one by one. A ghost by his side. Or that she had engineered it herself, and he tried to remember how many pills were in the box downstairs, whether it was enough. How could he be such a fool? Of course she would try again.

But then he sensed again the warmth of her. Knew her to be here still.

He wondered if he smelled unpleasant and tried to recall the last time he changed his t-shirt and underwear. A few days ago. He no longer owned a washing machine and didn't frequent the laundrette in the village more than once a month. You didn't notice what you became used to. He owned so few clothes anyway. He made a mental note to visit one of the shops in the village if she stayed for longer.

The dog stretched and gave a half moan, as if it was any other morning, the recent changes of no consequence. It remained by the girl's side, perhaps out of a sensed vulnerability. As a protector? He'd heard they did this, and his respect for it returned. It must have come upstairs with her in the night, a shepherding of sorts.

Again he tried to inch the bedding back across her.

She had been cold, he said to himself. That was it. So cold once the fire had finished that she came to his bed, sharing body heat like a pair trapped on a mountain might. The gesture was simply a pragmatic one; he'd been stupid to think otherwise.

And yet.

He'd forgotten how the world could do this, conjure its absurd magic. A girl he'd seen in the sea from his window, three mornings later furled into the back of him, the space between them almost nothing. Just when you thought there were rules, that one day resembled all others, a seismic jolt struck the ground you stood on. Like when he went to prison or his brother fell. His mother.

Another urge: to push back into her, just a fraction, but knowing that he mustn't.

Finally, the rhythm of her breathing found him, tiny heaves up against his back, and he knew this was as good a moment as any he'd had in life. A moment expanding and contracting, filling with endless possibilities, both a beginning and an end, a juncture. And in that moment he knew he was done with the yard.

He tried to mirror her breathing, as if harmony would yield a union. From its barely audible inhalation, to the minis- cule pause at its height, and the slightly laboured exhale. He broke it down to ever-smaller parts, imagined he was breathing for her, as he had on the beach, her mouth then cool and pliant, briny. The same mouth as it was now, and yet repeating the action when she woke would be incalculably different. He wanted to quell the thoughts, as he had those of the yard, but their encroachment was irresistible. They found their way, like water, back to you. Again he wondered where they began, how something came from nothing. And yet he knew something could not come from nothing.

His mouth on hers, he thought again. The breath, stay with the breath.

Seven years, he figured, since he'd shared a bed, and then only in habit. An area of the mattress between him and his wife, like a fissure, their bodies only colliding in accident, objects brushing against each other like passing jetsam. A time before that, of intimacy he supposed, though he could hardly recall one. He'd come with baggage, for sure, enough for the both of them. He recalled even on his wedding day looking at her, thinking: You too will leave. Everybody does. And yet she didn't, not for a long while. Not until there was a daughter to take as well.

The day he walked out of the prison, it was not beyond hope that someone might be there to meet him. That his letters had been read, forgiveness found. A driving test recently passed, his daughter parked across the road, the start of a new chapter. Or his father, having somehow learned of the date, standing at the gate, ready to make amends.

The girl stuttered in her in-breath, like something catching on the wind, and he followed the flow until it evened out.

That you are here, he kept saying in his head, is astonishing.

He longed for their clothes to be absent, wanted to feel her skin on his back. To circle the burn marks she'd made on her arm, heal them. To trace her birthmark with his finger. He felt a cough rising, suppressed it, returned to his own breath. A gull's cry shifted something in her and he wondered if he should speak, so she wasn't shocked on waking.

He wanted her to read to him in her own language, induce

in him a torpor as her tongue troubled each soft syllable. They could read to one another by the fire every evening - this is where they would connect, as storytellers. In time he would tell her about Blue, about his mother.

But if nothing else, he thought, then this is enough. More than enough.

He tried to figure out the time. He sensed from the girl's shallow breath that she was awake. Her body had stiffened a little and he waited for the commotion.

You were cold? he finally said.

She withdrew her arm, though not as a flinch, the rest of her unmoving.

It's OK, he continued. You still need to keep warm. I can put more wood on the fire tonight.

She edged back a few inches in the bed, and he reciprocated. The absence of her warmth was like a grief.

I will make some breakfast, he said, though he remained there, as if needing her words first, to confirm that food wasn't absurd right now, which was how it seemed to him. The tide would be out for a few hours yet and he thought about suggesting a walk after they had eaten, if her foot was up to it. Just a little way, so she could get some air.

You should get out this morning, he said, then realised how this could sound, despite her good English. For a walk, I mean, along the beach. With the dog.

The other direction, he almost added, away from the spot you went in.

Perhaps it was too soon for the beach; they could always head inland, pick up the path that led to the woods. He'd not been there since; had never had the courage. For years he'd fantasised of taking a chainsaw to the tree, propelling the machine's teeth deep into the flesh, undoing all its majesty, its stature, send it crashing like Blue to the ground. How old was it, he wondered. A hundred years, perhaps more. The events of that day would be barely a footnote in its history. But over time his anger towards the tree had diminished and his feeling had shifted; he'd imagined it cradling his brother for as long as it could, giving him up only after great effort. Perhaps he could return to the site after all, especially now that he had someone to accompany him.

Again he thought about talking to Anca about the water, her attempt, but he knew he lacked the words. There'd been a couple of suicides in prison, young men, newly sentenced, their potential for self-harm missed. There was a contempt for such people, their supposed cowardice, passing on all their anguish to someone else. Perhaps he should tell her this, that it spared no one. That the burden left for those behind was unyielding.

Or we can go into the village, he said.

The girl hummed her approval and he wanted her to replace her arm now that the talking had finished. Just for another few minutes. Instead she eased out of bed and he heard her on the stairs.

HIS SMELL WAS different, somehow elemental, and it reminded her more of the women at the farm than the men who visited the parlour. A scent that evoked the natural state of things: of sea and wood smoke and toil. Nothing adulterated. It would be unpleasant to some, rank even. It was how she imagined her father smelled after a day in the fields, her mother too perhaps – all the particulate matter of the landscape on them, their clothes and skin and hair, secreting in folds. How all people had once smelled.

She had woken to an insistent, spiking cold, disorientated again by the unfamiliar shadows, the room unknown for a few seconds until her mind caught up. Her bedding lay on the floor, the dog half on it, and she saw the fire had gone out. Yet still the sense of a sanctuary for the first time in more than a year, a place the terror could start to diminish.

The house was quiet compared to the barn and she realised there was loneliness in silence, despite the awfulness of the farm, and wondered how someone lived here alone. He had the dog, she supposed, and perhaps visitors.

She remembered the sea, its own cold beyond description, and yet it had this magnetism to it, as if she would now always need to be near it. And coming in waves of its own, the shame, rising in her like a tirade. She knew it was a mortal sin to remove what was sacred, what was created in His image. No suffering, they had been taught, justified it: the judgement of our lives His business alone. And yet where had He been during those acts committed against her? When she had reached out into the blackness and prayed for intervention, a sign that the evil gorging of her had some purpose, some end-point? Violation after violation, her body ravaged and plundered, subject to hate and indifference and callousness. He will never abandon you, their priest used to say. He will see you safely through this life, though silence was all she heard. Silence and the thought that He, the giver of all life, had also created those men brutalising her.

And if He was in our bodies, as well as our souls, hadn't He too suffered all the pillaging of her? Hadn't their deeds defiled Him also, subjected Him to the same degradation? But no, she had not felt His presence, the burden she knew was hers alone.

In that room at the parlour she learned in time to yield her body, offer it as one might an unloved toy, the detachment achieved by conjuring image after vivid image, of a land she believed she'd grown weary of, a childhood basking in the medieval foothills of Carpathia, with its ceaseless streams and waterfalls, spruce-flanked canyons and stoical mountains. They'd learned at school how the region had always resisted would-be conquerors: Romans, Huns, Slavs and Saxons, all defeated by the terrain.

Dreams of freedom began to sustain her, becoming embroiled with the unspoilt landscape of home, its high alpine meadows thick with the scent of juniper bushes and daffodils. This was where she went to in her mind. To see again the wild orchids, hear the first cuckoos. Dancing all day to shepherds' songs, whilst fiddlers played in rivalry to the birds of the forest.

You never knew a place until you left it.

Yet even after escaping the farm there had been no reclamation of her body, this husk she dragged around, tainted
and beyond purging. Why shouldn't she finish what they had
begun? What punishment in the after-world could mimic the
last year in this one?

She had changed her mind, though, in those last moments,
but was exhausted, and the sea was strong and swift. From
deep within her she had found a strength she thought lost. A
deep-rooted dignity and courage that perhaps all the women
of her family possessed – perhaps all women – as if it took the
awesome might of the sea to draw it from her.

You may take my body but you cannot take me.

There should have been no reprieve though; dusk had afforded her the privacy required to slip unnoticed into the
water. He'd seen her go in, she supposed, perhaps from this
very room, and moments later had found her and pulled her
ashore. A miracle, her mother would have termed it. An angel
from above.

And what of her parents' faith? How had this survived
their daughter's disappearance? Was it a source of comfort
when the weeks became months? Or were their prayers also
met with His silence? Their mother's belief, she suspected,
would only have hardened, perhaps their father's too, though
more from a sense of compliance. But she hoped doubt had
permeated her brother's heart, the blind obedience undone
forever.

She recalled the small village church at home, its bleached
stuccoed walls rising towards heaven, the air inside agitated
only by birdsong and the incessant scritch of insects. How
sunlight fell across them. She rarely listened to the dreary

homilies, instead losing herself to the beauty of the building itself, a stillness that was hypnotising. But once she was old enough to decide, and to her mother's disgust, she stopped going. In the early days of the parlour she'd thought what the men did to her a punishment for her lapsed attendance and had begged for clemency.

Earlier she had tried to reclaim the blankets without disturbing the dog, but the animal held firm and it became a sort of game. At the fireplace she positioned some small bits of wood on the ashes and blew. Nothing. There were no logs and she had no desire to search outside in the darkness. She got dressed and stood at the window, sensing more than seeing the vastness of water. It agitated her to not know where in this country she was. South and west, she'd learned, but beyond that only disorientation. She thought of animals and birds that could navigate home on instinct, their primal compass laid down before birth. Even were the sea becalmed and a boat replete with supplies offered, it would be beyond her to know which direction to sail. She was still a prisoner.

As her eyes adjusted, a cresting wave appeared, as if being drawn by hand. The sea's white noise had been an irritant initially, a humiliation even, taunting her failure, but it was a source of comfort now, like a lullaby, soothing her in the fragmented nights.

THE STAIRS SEEMED to groan under her weight and with each step she expected him to appear. On the landing she saw the dog had followed her and she gave a silent plea for it to be quiet. The corridor on the first floor went in both directions, but the only room she knew was the bathroom. Taking small steps, her ankle tender yet clearly healing, she paused outside each open door until she heard a faint snore. Standing there she could hear the wind and felt the house heave a little as if breathing itself.

The room was darker than downstairs, despite the absence of curtains, and she waited for a minute until her eyes became accustomed enough to get a feel for its layout. She followed the sound of his breath to work out the position of the bed.

The women at the farm rarely slept quietly; fitful nights were spent as you waited for someone else to cry out with whatever images their dreams served up. If it was someone nearby, you would offer comfort, gently wake them, mollify them back into sleep, and hope that in turn someone would be there for you. But here there was nothing beyond the elements, and this gentle breathing of a man who'd saved her from drowning.

She inched towards the bed, felt its edge with her knee, patted with her hands to check which side he was. And then, as though it was nothing out of the ordinary, she lifted the bedding and eased herself in beside him. He didn't move, his breathing remaining regular, and she lay as still as possible.

Why she did this, she didn't know, and she tried not to think of all the unspeakable things done to her. He is not like them, she told herself.

The bed was cold, but she could sense warmth coming from him. She heard the dog settle on the floor behind her, as if it had corralled her here and was encouraging her to stay. Still this need, not just for warmth, she realised, but for contact. Like the women at the farm had offered, their absence keenly felt. That need to be held, cradled. Connected with another.

She tried to reduce the space between them imperceptibly, like a shadow shifting as the sun passed over.

Images of the men formed and she fought to banish them. Spitting, biting, slobbering over her like dogs. Pummelling. Never content with the angle or tempo. Declarations of adoration, followed by contempt when they finished. What is it in your nature that needs this, she would think, that can subject another to such things? She was providing a service, they were often told, as if the men were cars.

Lying there she ran a finger across the scar tissue on her arm, traversing the crenulations the cigarette had made. She counted to ten and then reached out. Her hand found fabric and she realised it was his clothing. She'd considered this, that he might be naked, and had fought down the terror. Her fingers applied a sequence of light brushes strokes, as if assessing whether something was hot or not. Several minutes passed and she gently laid a hand on his back, hoping that sleep would come.

In the morning he suggested leaving the house. They walked slowly, the dog out ahead, orbiting them in drawn out ellipses, eager to prolong the outing. It was strange to feel so little, as if the sea had closed down the part of her prone to emotion. Or perhaps Hallam's presence reassured her, though he was not a big man. She could see the village along the coast, perhaps a kilometre away, the place she'd been given a lift to after escaping. A small lorry, its driver taking pity as she cowered into a hedge near the farm.

She could scarcely belief it when none of them had been around that day, except the kind one, and he'd stopped watching her so closely. They'd spoken of escape, the other women and her, from time to time, but no one knew how you survived beyond the farm without money or documents. She at least spoke some English. But there were the rumours of what happened to the ones who tried and were caught. Why make life harder still, went the wisdom. Pay off what was owed and they would let you go. She wondered how many of them truly believed this, that once they had settled the debt, or when they could no longer work in the fields or the parlour, that freedom awaited and they could return home or to a life less degrading. For surely once their worth expired they became a burden, fit only for the bottom of a ditch on the farm's outskirts. Either way, she wasn't going to wait to see. And when the one who'd given her pills and chocolate was left alone that morning, she accepted the invitation to flee.

The few women who hadn't gone to the fields tried to dissuade her, but on seeing her resolve their eyes burned with a vicarious thrill. Taking turns, they hugged her, a couple handing her some small token as a keepsake: coins they'd found around the farm, a piece of jewellery that had escaped the men's attention.

There was still an hour or so before the van left for the

parlour, the man telling her to be ready and to have some food first. She watched through the gap in the barn door as he walked back to the main house and checked again that the other vehicles had all gone. She took her chance, flanked the barn walls, ducked beneath the windows of the house, and walked out. For long seconds she expected him to call out, to emerge from the gate in pursuit. Even along the road she waited for the van's engine rising up behind her, the familiar crunch of gears as it picked up speed.

But it never did.

After half an hour of steady walking, she found a busier road, cars zipping past her, their drivers staring hard but not stopping. It was raining by the time the lorry stopped, the man leaning out the cab, asking if she was alright. She thought how wretched she must look and assumed that the driver would ask for payment in return for giving her a lift, and that if she refused, he would take it anyway.

Where are you going? he said and all she could do was point the way the road went.

He spoke several times but she merely nodded and smiled awkwardly, waiting for the subject of recompense to come up. Perhaps, she thought, she could do it one last time in order to get far enough away. In the end though, she opened the door and jumped out at some traffic lights, running back to a gateway as fast as she could.

They neared the village, Hallam and her, and the shed that had been her home for several nights. The wind was up more here, the gulls brazen, landing and sauntering up to inspect litter, barely moving aside for them or the dog. She noticed he'd trimmed his beard a little since they woke, and how this took some years off him. His hair needed tidying and she wondered if he'd let her cut it later, as she once had her brother's and father's.

She wanted to ask him about the house, how he came to be there. There was this childlike urge in her to explore all its rooms now that she was mobile, imagining the place full of life.

We can cut inland, he said, there are some woods.

She thought for a moment, remembering the looks she'd got from locals a few days ago.

Can we walk that way, she said, to see the village. He seemed relieved.

He called the dog to heel and they headed past the first houses. Villagers drifted back and forth, contending with the stiff breeze. She supposed they looked an odd couple by any standards, and she took a strange delight from people's stares this time, holding eye contact until they turned away.

This is my friend, she felt like saying. I'm staying in his house on the cliff.

She wanted to go into the shops and buy the food she'd stared at forlornly a few days before.

It gets busy here in the summer, Hallam said. The tourists.

She liked when he did this, when the silence forced him to idly chat as if he were embarrassed. Perhaps later, after supper, she would tell him everything. She thought about his age, the same as her dad's she guessed, maybe a little younger. There were three photographs above the fire in the room where she slept, and she vowed to ask about them. In one a woman in her early forties laughed raucously, a cigarette held with lavish effect, a glass of wine aloft in her other hand. The second was of a boy, a teenager, uncomfortably captured by the lens though not shy. She sensed they were related and wondered where they were now. The final picture was a girl in school uniform only a few years younger than she was. Every time she looked at it, she remembered what she had lost.

They reached the harbour, the dog excited by the familiar fishermen, some of whom nodded to Hallam before eyeing her briefly. Yes, she thought, this is the way all men look at me. At home it had been a cause for delight, boys noticing her for the first time and knowing she could perhaps have her choice.

They spoke for a while, the men and Hallam, staring out to sea, Hallam looking down onto the boats. Perhaps he could sail her home, teach her how to navigate the high seas, the two of them and the dog, buccaneers on a voyage across oceans. Home.

P RISON CALCIFIES THE heart. It reduces you to
base needs – food, survival, safety. Everything else is shut
down. This is how you endure.

He'd accepted his punishment early on; he knew it to be
just. He was swift to learn the rules for coping, a code to
observe: who to speak to, who not to, a blade forthcoming if
you got it wrong. But you could not opt out of violence alto-
gether; like the wind, it came your way every now and then.
For many inmates it was an instrument of power more than a
means to an end, simple animalistic displays to establish your
place in the order. You might hear a rumour that a reckoning
was due, and often, once you knew it was coming, it was
better to go in first, go in hard with all the shock you had, to
not stop until they'd seen you had something about you, that
you wouldn't roll over. This is what I am prepared to do, it
said, and he thought of Blue on these occasions. Sometimes
it worked, you were left alone. Mostly it didn't. He'd known
real violence as an adult only once, and then as its distribu-
tor, and so those first times inside were like a sickness you'd
not encountered before. There was no fear, though, which he
found curious, and he figured that the guilt took care of this.
I deserve this, he told himself. I had it coming.

In his cell at night he often pondered when the first human
violence occurred. As soon as people encountered one another,
he guessed, as soon as resources required protecting. Weapons

hewn from a need to triumph next time, arms races from sticks to bombs. Tribal violence, then. Fathomable. But beyond this, when did humans clash over something other than food or property or religion, driven instead by some inner rage not fully understood, by love or jealousy or malfunction. Or through violence for its own sake, the only goal to do harm, to inflict damage on another.

Violence in prison marked itself apart from brawls he'd witnessed in the real world by its speed. There was none of the posturing and bravado, no men held back by others, shoving, shouting, to-ing and fro-ing. It was swift and efficient, like a bird of prey, over in seconds, the devastation total nonetheless.

It never occurred to him that he might be the sort of person who went to prison. As if the categories were precise, without crossover. His brother, yes, he could imagine that as a teenager. All Blue's fire and obduracy, rising to conflict rather than shying away from it. It would only take the right situation, a touch-paper. His own fuse, though, had just been longer, slower to burn.

There is someone else, his wife had said in that other time, as if announcing she had to work late, or that their daughter had skipped school. She spoke in a neutral tone with an undercurrent of menace.

Someone else, he had repeated.

I'm sorry.

He let the silence gather.

Say something, she said. You must have known.

And he realised he had, or that some part of him had worked it out, like a tic you've had for a while but only just acknowledged.

He looked away and could feel his wife's stare, the hard bit done, the first words uttered, and now she wanted to explain, so he let her. She described his moods and the distance it fashioned between them, how he wouldn't let her in, that he lived in the past. She'd said this a lot over the years, but he never understood how you stopped thinking about what had gone, and how when he'd tried, it only made the focus sharper. You couldn't think about the future, as it was unknown, and the present seemed too slippery a thing to grasp. But he let her say all these things and supposed there was a truth in them.

Her voice rose and fell, faltered and flowed through tears and snot, and every now and then she would hit him, not hard, more a shove to the chest, as she pleaded for him to react, to take ownership of what was playing out, like she'd been the one wronged. Hit me harder, he wanted to say.

Instead he returned his mind to the woods, walking alongside his brother, whose swagger alone kept the others from him, how it must have been hardwired in Blue to protect him, and he wondered whether he would have done the same had he been the elder. Whenever he met someone new in life, he was minded to tell them about his brother in the first few minutes, and his wife had been no exception. Not because it was a morbid story, but he figured it was a way of giving Blue a little more life. I wish you could have met him, he tended to say, the listener confused at the lack of segue. He'd wait a while before talking about his mother, and he could see the fear in people's faces when he did; their concern that it might be inherited. It must have sounded like a family curse.

His wife was still speaking now, about the ghosts in him, the drinking, that she wouldn't let him drag them under too. It was a cruel phrase, the dragging under bit, and a few days later he wondered if she had chosen it deliberately, and he'd wanted to confront her.

Don't you want to know who it is, she asked, but he hadn't, not at first.

It made sense, he recalled thinking, it was just another event along the arc of his life. As if her infidelity was preordained, blame inappropriate. But it festered anyway, somewhere in the gut, radiating outwards until it took all of him.

Perhaps sensing this, his wife's desire for honesty receded. That it had happened was all he needed to know, she said, that she was leaving. The other man was a symptom, she added, not the cause of anything. She was not in love with this person, they had no future either. He was a catalyst, that was all.

Why hadn't that been enough for him? For him to dismiss this man as incidental. A small component part in the engine of his doomed marriage.

He believed her, that she wasn't replacing him, wasn't abandoning him, as his father had, for another lover. But he could not stop the images of their union, over and over they played, sound, smell, colour, looping until he had no other thought. Several times in those days he vomited, always at the point he pictured the man entering her, or when she took him in her mouth. Not knowing details became its own haunting, and he would guess as to their geometry together, their configuration, the imagination a cruel editor. Only he couldn't see half of it, half of them.

This faceless form, and at first he wanted to meet the man only to give him substance, to remove the power of the unknown. But the longer his anonymity prevailed, the more the man became a symbol for all his losses. He imagined his wife's lover in Blue's tree, in the water with his mother that

156

day. The man was the woman their father could not let go of, the bullies at school. He was the father who left them. He was the god who divined it all.

It was hard to trace someone with no starting point, and this too had its supremacy over him, his impotency mocked a second time. He watched and waited, observed his wife's life with forensic scrutiny. Replayed in his mind her movements of the previous months, documented her habits, the obsession sustaining him on some level. She'd stated the affair was over and he believed her; there was no sense she might lead him to the man now. The weeks slipped by, days taut like wire, his wife, he assumed, making provision for a departure.

In the end it was their daughter who gave the man up. A chance anecdote at the dinner table, about a teacher who'd helped her with revision, who'd gone beyond the norm to bring his subject to life, that the tuition had come to a premature end, how she was disappointed. It was an innocuous remark, meant to break the silence that had formed since the revelation, their daughter like a fraying rope attempting to stop two ships from drifting apart. But it was his wife's face that told him, the mention of the man's name causing it to bloom and flush, her extended downward gaze giving her away.

When he found the man he took to watching him, across a road from his daughter's school, followed him to a house, watched some more. Like observing a creature in the wild, all this curiosity and wanting not to be seen. There was this plainness to him he hadn't expected, unremarkable clothes, a face that was neither ugly nor handsome. Older too than he had anticipated. He lived alone, as far as Hallam could tell, had no family, was betraying no one. For a week he watched him, feeling nothing at first, a routine of sorts, as if reclaiming something. And then observing his wife later with this new power.

He wondered if he wanted to see them together, to announce himself then, but his wife had been true to her word, the union apparently suspended, and he thought he detected some sadness in the man's face as he came and went.

There was no planning, no thinking ahead. Just this instinct to enter the man's house, occupy his territory, and he followed him to the front door one afternoon, timed it so they arrived together.

A strange politeness came from the man, even once he knew, and he invited Hallam in, as if some mature exchange was to be had. The man made some tea, asked about Hallam's daughter, said how much potential was there. He talked some more, fumbled things, made no eye contact.

Hallam wanted to find his own words, but none came, and at that point he thought he might leave. As if that was the next thing that should occur. But then all the things life had put on him gathered and rose in him, and he could see that the man knew it as well.

It surprised him, how he could function on this mechanical level, and there was this great release in the violence, like a hosepipe that had been long kinked. Punches, kicks, stamps. He stopped, but only once all the water had come out. The man offered nothing in return, had let the blows land again and again, barely protecting himself, the politeness continuing even then.

He sat next to the man afterwards, a calmness he'd not felt before, his own hands bleeding gently, spotting into the larger area of blood that formed on the kitchen floor.

Are you alive? he heard himself say, and after a while he fetched a cushion for the man's head, eased him on to it. It's OK, he said, and the man groaned like he was drunk.

After calling the ambulance he stayed next to him, soothed his head as he had done Blue's.

Neither his wife nor daughter came to the trial, and the house they'd all rented together had been full of a new family when he returned to it after his release. Staying with friends, was the conspiratorial reply from neighbours. And then, abroad for a break, his solicitor told him, and then remaining there. He could challenge it, his daughter not yet an adult, but he'd need money. His conviction would count against him. Let her come back in her own time, came the counsel.

He'd always planned to write to her, once Seafield was improved. Invite her to visit, to stay. It was shame, he supposed, that kept her away. At what he'd done. That he was this person she didn't know. Who could hurt her teacher so badly.

THE GIRL WAS going through the kitchen cupboards. He'd bought some chicken and vegetables after their walk, accepted her offer to cook dinner later. He watched as she gathered ingredients, humming to herself. They'd gone in a shop earlier, and he'd wanted to find something for tonight, a new shirt or jumper, to mark it as different. In the end the gesture had seemed excessive. Instead they'd walked down to the harbour and it surprised him, the absence of awkwardness now. A niece visiting, he'd have said, though no one asked, and he wondered what Blue's children might have been like.

Got anything? he'd asked by the boats, meaning work, knowing he'd need it soon, but not wanting to appear desperate. The dog was all giddy around the men, submissive, the girl laughing at it. If she speaks, he thought, they'd know they weren't related. How could he say he pulled her from the sea? That he was looking after her? He watched them trying not to look at her, stealing little stares anyway, and he felt all paternal or something near this.

If the weather clears, one of them said, we'll need someone to come out tomorrow.

He nodded, said he'd come down early to see. A trip out could feed him and the girl for a week, maybe longer. A day every now and then was all he needed, until something else came along. He pictured being out on the boat in the morning, felt this wave of pleasure.

The yard owner would have lost patience by now and he imagined the words used about him. They'd expect him to collect his gear in time – goggles and gauntlets he'd had since his training. Perhaps he'd leave his stuff there, not chance the fall-out. It was about looking forward now, not back. He would call the developers tomorrow, see what their best offer for Seafield was.

He left the girl to it, got some wood in. He thought there was a bottle of wine somewhere, instead of the whisky, though only tumblers to drink it from. Wine was OK, he told himself, a social drink. It was the ones you drank alone you had to watch.

His mother would have been appalled at his poor hosting, and he imagined the house had she been entertaining someone. Music wending from room to room, riding on glorious aromas of some culinary delight. Nothing left to chance. There was no excuse for being an inadequate host, she would say, whatever turmoil was going on behind the scenes. Even with Blue wired up and his father long gone, there was a veneer of indulgence with her.

He'd been living with his father's new family a couple of months when the call came, his brother's deterioration quicker than expected, an infection journeying to his lungs, antibiotics largely ineffectual. Driving down, his father was silent, save the occasional trite line, of it being for the best, and he wondered how this was true, whether his father ushered all tragedy through this filter.

At least he didn't know about your mother, his father said, yet Hallam knew that he did, that his words had permeated

161

Blue's mind, like water percolating down into the ground. And this being Blue's choice now, to join her.

You mean doesn't, he said, angry at his father's using the past tense. At least he doesn't know.

They parked up and his father put an arm on him, and this the last contact they would have, Hallam saying it to himself, marking it.

Come on, he said, let's go see your brother.

The building itself had this great hush to it, like a snowy copse, their footfall drawing exaggerated attention to itself. At the reception his father made an attempt at humour with the woman, and in that moment he saw all his inadequacy. His fraudulence.

Blue appeared no different. Just as in those seconds after his fall, all the foulness and undoing lay hidden behind his exterior. His skin was perhaps a shade more pallid, as if mimicking the leaching of their mother, his eyes sunken like pebbles in the snow. But still that unruly fop of hair and he imagined the nurses lovingly washing it, attempting in vain to style it.

Hallam approached the bed, glanced at a screen's readings he supposed had led to their summoning. Oxygen flowed into his brother, bolstering the frail inhalations. He wanted his own moment, absent of their father, and in the end he had to ask for this final vigil.

You look all hollowed out, he thought, as if the electricity in his brother had begun its leaving.

The words they were given by staff didn't register with him, a conversation he was encouraged to be present for, and then another he was not. He watched his father fill out a form, the pen failing then working again, the staff comforting him. A sheet of paper, he thought. His brother's life determined by this. And then a powering down. Like an android. And the building even quieter, Blue no longer between worlds.

We can stop and get fish and chips, his father said on the way back. That new one across town. As if life came in chapters. His step-mother giving him this dutiful hug when they got home.

You can stay off school tomorrow, his father said, his new siblings sheepish in their approach.

Blue had joined their mother's ashes in the commemorative garden at the crematorium, where they remained until Hallam moved back after prison. A polite gathering of the dead, un-remarkable, communal.

I've come for my mother and my brother, he told the man in the office that day. Another form and he was allowed to take them away, where they sat like sacred artefacts in his rucksack as he walked to the house along the cliff edge. Several people passed him on the path, his cargo emitting a conspiratorial energy on his back, three instead of one, and he felt briefly empowered by this. For he believed something remained of them, an elemental residue. Calcium. Carbon. Potassium. Matter even a furnace cannot break down.

A week later he chose a spot for them, set back from the coast path, elevated so that it took in Seafield, the island on the horizon, all the sea in between. He thought to say something, wished he'd planned it better.

The powder of them dispersed in the wind, took to the earth and rock around him, and he allowed the remnants to settle on his hands until it too gusted to nothing.

THE MAN PARKED the van in a side road, felt the beer and weed interacting, a fusion in the blood that, done in precise quantities, calibrated him without the need for anything stronger. The boy hadn't spoken much since lunch, though his colour had returned. There would be some backlash from their punishing the English broker, but the family name would be emboldened by it in the long run. They'd left the man half-dead and he knew the skill in this, the timing of when to stop. Only once had he got it wrong, back home. It wasn't a science.

Before arriving here, they'd explored a little the coast a few miles away, found a quiet cove that could serve them well, made a note of its GPS for those bringing the gear in. Less than an hour back to the farm. There was a disused jetty too and he congratulated himself as he rehearsed telling his cousin.

See, I get things done, he imagined saying.

Half an hour's drive and they were now in the village where there'd been a sighting, a girl with an accent. A fool's errand, it likely was, another phrase he'd got to know. At least he could say they tried, and as the day had deepened, more of him was pleased the girl had got away, despite the headache it had caused. Had the boy not been along he would have made something up, that he heard she'd gone north, or he'd found her in some squat, overdosed, no use to anyone. Now he'd have to look for real, go through the motions.

When they'd come out of the pub at lunchtime, the boy had got his cockiness back, perhaps the beer, perhaps because of the beating he'd given out. He had tried telling the boy they would head north to the coast, to look for a landing site, and then return home. But the boy had brought up the matter of the girl, as if this was their main purpose to the day, and he realised now why his cousin had sent his son with him. Not at all as an apprentice, but more to keep an eye on him, to ensure this last task wasn't neglected. A test of loyalty, then.

And so they were here, to chase a ghost.

He observed the people busying back and forth, like cattle, and he recalled the cows in his village at home, how they would take themselves to pasture each morning, returning as a herd at dusk, where they would peel off one by one into their respective properties. Tourists marvelled at the spectacle of it, but it disgusted him, reminded him of everything he refused to be.

The boy started skinning up and he gave him a half punch to the arm, shook his head.

Use your brain, he said, and the boy muttered something, then put it away.

Outside the air was fresher than on the farm, as if the sea was in it, and he thought how you'd feel cleaned out by it after a while. The wind pushed hard along the narrow streets, the salt on it turning his stomach a little, and he thought to tell the boy to go ahead with the weed after all.

The roads were stupidly narrow here and they had to step into a doorway every time a vehicle passed. A series of sharp cries fell on them and he braced for violence until he saw a pair of gulls squabbling overhead, the noise amplified by houses with first floors that overhung.

Vermin, he said to the boy, aiming an imaginary gun at the birds.

People passed them, smiling, some saying hello, and he had no idea what to make of it, why strangers thought this was OK to do, like they were family. They passed a pub, saw a fire working hard in the corner, and the boy suggested it, now that he had a taste for the beer here.

You're working, he told him like a boss would, but thinking that it was a good idea. Instead they walked around for an hour, like being on a holiday, he thought, and laughing he told the boy to get himself an ice cream, could see he was fed up.

They went in a few of the shops, made up this story about their sister having got lost, that she always did, wandering off, not all there, as they said over here.

A few days ago, he continued. That she had no money, knew nobody. But no one had seen her and he felt this disgust at them for their politeness, wanted to give them a reason to dislike him.

Instead he took out the roll of cash from his pocket, started peeling some notes back.

Skinny, he said. Skinny and pretty. About this tall.

He described what she was wearing when he'd seen her leave the farm, and by now his patience was almost gone. He said her name, just in case, then put the money away.

He tried hard to picture her, more for himself now than these people, found that he couldn't get her all. He remembered the birthmark on the side of her, how his cousin had made her show them that first day, a parade. And he could picture the burn marks made down her arm, like a branding,

166

that time she refused to go to the parlour. How he'd nearly intervened, to stop his cousin. But the details of her face had flown.

Outside the shop the boy was speaking about the girl, taunted him for losing her, like he'd heard the others at the farm do, thinking that he carried the same weight as his father.

You shouldn't be so careless, the boy said. We won't find her now.

Around the corner, once they were out of sight, he grabbed the boy's cock and balls, forced him into the wall. With his other hand he rotated hard one of the boy's ears, feeling that with a little more force he could remove it, like tearing the pelt off a rabbit, and he knew the sound it would make. He pressed his face hard into the boy's, kept it there, easing the pressure of his hands a little, then gripping more.

When the screams matched the gulls, he let him go, brushed him down like an accident had occurred, a simple misunderstanding. He placed an open hand on the boy's cheek, patted it. He had to judge it right, so it wouldn't get back, but there needed to be this respect there.

They cut back through some side streets, got lost for a minute, then found the right way. He felt a little bad, knew sometimes he went too far, suggested they went in the pub after all, where he ordered them beer and vodka, the boy flinching when he sat next to him.

Come on, he said, clinking glasses. It's all forgotten. Drink these and we'll go. We can have a smoke on the way back. I was just messing. He got them more vodka, asked the barman if there'd been a foreign girl in, so the boy could see him doing it.

When they emerged the wind had dropped, the village less fraught, and he felt this homesickness. The smell of the sea, he thought, it was on you so quickly. The last time he had been on a small boat he'd puked the whole time, and he felt relief he wouldn't be the one bringing the drugs in.

They headed back past the shops they'd gone in, a few closing up now, owners giving them a look, like they were the wrong kind of outsiders now. Not the kind who spent money.

The light was still just about there, perhaps another half-hour or so, the days here so short this time of year. He gave the boy a friendly punch to the arm, got a nervous laugh from him, the drink taking off the edginess from before.

They were heading back to the van – they'd be home by the fire in an hour or so – when the boy pointed to a couple of fishermen on the quayside, sluicing down the deck of a boat.

THE FOOD LOOKED bland and he placed the salt by her, hoped she wasn't offended. He couldn't find any wine and it felt too early for the whisky. It was good to be cooked for and he had loitered as she made it, wanting to be useful, or perhaps just to witness it. He got the radio to some station without pop music or talking.

In the lounge, after getting the fire up, he found two candles, lit them and allowed wax to fall on the coffee table, held them there until it solidified. He wished there was a dining table, so they didn't have to eat on their laps, or kneel on the floor.

He asked again if she needed help and she issued a playful rebuke.

This was not nothing, he thought. All too often he only noticed the shifting into a new phase once it had passed, and it felt strange to observe it in real time. He'd resisted speaking of the bed, their sharing of it last night, and she hadn't brought it up. After dinner he would say it was OK, if she wanted to again, to keep warm. There was no pressure, their own designated sides.

He allowed his mind to bask a little in the memory of this morning, tried to summon the sensation of her arm on him, the softness of her breath.

In the long run he could fix up one of the other rooms for her. Not Blue's or his mother's. The least damaged guest room. They could get a bed from somewhere, decorate together. In occasional elaborate fantasies he imagined them running Seafield together, as a guesthouse again, its precariousness a novelty attraction, visitors knowing they could be the last person to occupy a room before the cliff beneath it fell away.

Above all he hoped she would read to him tonight, as she had that first day from one of his mother's books, and he wondered where this infantile desire formed, how he would make such a request. He hardly cared which one, longed only to lie in the cradle of her voice as sleep came for him. The rises and falls of her recital, stumbling occasionally on a word she didn't know how to pronounce, passing the book to him. They could alternate chapters, devour an entire novel in the coming days. He recalled reading to his daughter, wondered how so much time got behind you. And further back, surely his parents too had shuttered the day in such fashion, though he had no memory of this.

Earlier, when they returned from the walk, Anca had taken a bath. He'd suggested it, called down that he could run it for her, and she'd accepted the offer, like it was this ritual they had. The old tap had spluttered with the request for water, the pipes below clanking in protest for a few seconds. He heard the old boiler kick in downstairs, wondered if this novel demand would do for it.

She could probably shower now, he thought, but he was keen to demonstrate it was not all hardship here, that small luxuries could be had. Finally the water ran warm and he watched the level slowly rise up the cast iron sides. He wished there was something to make a layer of foam with, settled instead for opening a new soap for her, which he placed on a towel on the stool. He only thought of candles later, when he lit the ones at dinner.

When it was two thirds full he had called her, waited at the bottom of the stairs to hear her reaction, but she was silent. He heard the door close and for a moment was tempted to climb the staircase, stealthily, and listen for the sound her body made entering the water. She hadn't locked the door, he was sure – not that there was risk he'd enter – but it felt like a gesture nonetheless, this trust between them.

He recalled how there were bath nights here, twice a week, sometimes three, himself or Blue first in the water, then their mother, their father. Particularly dirty clothes would go in last, to soak before washing. He'd put the electric shower in himself, a few months after moving back, hadn't used the bath other than to catch the water.

He loitered from room to room, pausing in the hallway, listening to the small splashes her ablution made. The once-grand staircase that had seemed so magnificent as a teenager, coiling up through the core of Seafield, now a structure in need of repair. And then all too soon, the rush of water down the outflow pipe, the floorboards keening beneath her tread, and he pictured the towel cloaking her, remembered how he'd dried her hair after the sea.

They'd gone in the charity shop earlier, tying the dog up outside, and he'd watched her fan with her hand the rails of dresses and tops, made a note when she paused and removed one, held it against herself like a film-star. If they were back early from the fishing tomorrow, he'd go in and get one of them, leave it on the chair for her to find the next morning.

So he could wash her other clothes, he'd say.

He looked out the window now, watched the day shutting itself down. The sea was at its midpoint, last night's storm removing ample sand so that tips of the submerged oak forest could be glimpsed. He imagined a civilisation at its base, ossified as if rained on by pumice, frozen mid-deed, their bodies poised in work or play, in embrace. And then thousands of years later, his mother in the water above them, a circling angel.

Tomorrow he would rise before dawn, head down to the harbour, feel again the satisfaction in physical effort, the trawler chugging out beyond the breakwater, past the sandbar. The last stars would dwindle and light would slowly reveal itself and the world, and he'd look back at Seafield, knowing the girl was asleep in the bed, the dog nearby. The yard a thing barely remembered. He'd leave some money in the kitchen, imagined her walking into the village to buy bread, something for supper.

The boat would pitch and toss, and he'd find his sea legs after a while, the others teasing him. He would talk to the crew more, make this effort to not be an outsider. In time he could take the girl to the pub, introduce her. She'd need to find work soon and he wondered what she could do, what skills she had.

The trawler would head out past the island in the morning and he'd smile at all that paddling he and Blue did that day, his brother for once undone by exhaustion, like they'd crossed an ocean.

Twenty miles or so, they'd sail out tomorrow, beyond the bay, the coast just a frail band, out until the skipper got that feeling in his gut, or perhaps they had sonar now. Then the nets would go in and someone would brew tea, roll cigarettes, the skipper pushing the boat hard and there was this unspoken thrill.

Finally, they'd ease up, like the boat was out of breath. That was his favourite moment, a stillness, save the gentle rise and fall of the trawler, all that shared hope of activity below them, their powerlessness now. You didn't move unless you had to, made sure to keep your position. Such superstition, an ancient habit, he supposed, then a final prayer of sorts and they'd bring the nets in, just as people had always done. This great tension formed on the deck, knowing their fortunes rested on what came up, hoping the trawl held together, that the winches didn't burn out. It was still largely down to luck.

And then the first fish, nets alive with a silvered bounty, the men's eyes darting from each other's with relief. Taking it all in, gauging the extent of it, this mass of metallic scales. The smaller stuff was thrown back, monkfish and sole their hoped-for prize. No one spoke about stocks, about how long this was possible, not on the water, not when earning a living was this tight.

If he did well, there'd be longer trips, five, six days at sea, and he hoped the girl would look after the dog, be there when he got home, like a time from the past. He'd get some new boots after being paid, though new ones were never the same, and he wondered where his old ones were, how many nautical miles separated them.

After a while he'd ask the men about smaller boats, if they knew of any for sale. Line-fishing trips, he'd say, for tourists. Not a rival, although he'd have to make the boat pay in the winter. It was funny, how one shift brought about another, like you needed a push.

THE GIRL CALLED through and he longed to suspend it all, this actual moment, or to know there would be a hundred more like it. Earlier, walking along the seafront, he'd lingered half a pace behind her at times, watching the light snag in her hair, thought there something miraculous in this. She could leave now, he kept saying to himself, now she can walk. And yet she doesn't.

They ate at the coffee table, a couple of cushions for seats, the dog intrigued by it, the absence of height for the food. The radio had lost some of its signal and he got up to turn it off, worried about the silence.

It's fine, she said. Eat. And so he sat down.

He wanted to say about this thing, this quickening she made in him. So it would not become bottlenecked. Yet each rehearsal in his head was like a disembowelment, and instead they ate wordlessly, the candlelight flaming in her eyes whenever he could bring himself to look.

He would tell her about the prison time soon, what he'd done to his wife's lover, so it was out there and not a secret between them. Better she knew early on, so she could choose.

The noise was unfamiliar, in that it occurred so infrequently, and it took him a while to recognise it. The dog too seemed thrown by it, looking to Hallam as if for an explanation. One of the crew, he supposed, come to tell him he was no longer needed or that the weather had turned, and he cursed. This was why he would get his own boat, to not be dependent on others. It wasn't fair, to get a person's hopes up.

He left Anca and the food and opened the front door.

If the two men were crew, he hadn't seen them before. Their clothes weren't right either, for fishermen.

Alright, one of them said, and this thing rose in him, an instinct to close the door. It surprised him, that you could still know, like in prison. All the tiny cues to precede it. Again came the sense he was occupying a dream-state since pulling the girl from the water, a nether-reality, that this too was part of the trance.

He nodded but didn't speak, noticed the older one had this confidence to him. That he could look friendly without being it. The younger one couldn't have been more than a few years out of school, yet was the bigger of two, as if his body had outgrown him. Like a bull mutated by steroids.

She is a looker, no, the older one said, and there was this question in there, but more it was a statement. Too familiar, the tone was, for strangers and there was menace in this alone.

Again he said nothing, trying instead to weigh it all up, feeling there was no time to. The younger one was looking past him, into the house, so Hallam pulled the door a little towards him, tried to stand taller, as an animal would.

Our sister, the older one said. Run away, she has. Gets herself all worked up. Her mother is very worried.

The man's voice was like the girl's, he realised, harsher perhaps, but the same inflections, same modulation. She has family here after all, he thought, and wondered whether this made it better or worse, their connection to her.

There's no one else inside, he said, thinking they could

have been around the back anyway, looked in the windows. It's just me here.

This time the younger one spoke, more fretful than the first, agitated almost, and he thought, yes, you'll be the one to spark first.

She needs to come home, the younger one said. Tell her we're here to take her back.

There was silence then, a stillness holding all this energy between them, and he knew he couldn't take them both. He'd fought and beaten bigger men inside, but not two at once. He thought to fetch the girl, to see her reaction, see if she wanted to go with them. Perhaps that would appease them. Or tell them to return tomorrow, in the daylight, that he would speak to her in the meantime. It would be a reasonable request, given what she'd been through.

In the end the decision was taken from him, the younger one stepping forward with irregular speed, his fist from nowhere, and he fell back, holding the door handle to keep himself from going right down. A series of blows came – from both of them, it felt like – and he knew to stay up, that he was finished if he did not. He got an elbow away, into the side of one, but it was hopeless and soon he was down, curling into himself, trying to roll away and protect his head. Kicks this time and he heard the dog barking, heard it reaching them to join in the game, before a yelp and he sensed it retreating.

The blows finally diminished and he tried to calculate the damage, what he was capable of, whether there would be more. He remained still, to give out that he was finished, heard the men in the other room now, talking to the girl, one of them shouting, the younger one, it sounded like.

There were several sites of pain, but nothing debilitating,

and he thought of men in prison, how they never gave you this second chance. You didn't need to kill someone, just stop them coming back at you.

The girl's voice was raised now, beseeching, some English mixed with her own language. He managed to heft himself to sitting. A broken forearm perhaps, maybe a rib.

Again he thought to let them take her, knew it best to stay out of people's business, whatever it looked like. There was obviously a family dispute, the girl had fled. Perhaps there was no more to it. What right did he have to get involved?

He looked around the hallway for something to use, saw the dog cowering in a corner. There were knives in the kitchen but there was enough logic in him still, to know that risked prison. A gun was better, he supposed, as long as you didn't use it. You didn't argue with a gun.

He smeared the back of a hand across his face, felt the warm skein of blood from his nose, and there was a flash of that other time, his wife's lover pleading below him and his hardly recalling what he'd done. Get up, he had shouted, realised the man couldn't.

Pulling himself up with the banister, he edged along the wall and opened the door down to the workshop, tried to minimise its whine. The stairs too wanted to give him up and he used the rail to lighten his tread. Slow and shallow, he tried to make his breath, the rib catching where it shouldn't, his arm pulsing with a rhythm beyond pain.

There was more shouting upstairs, the men at each other or at the girl, he couldn't tell. He could hear something being broken, furniture shifted. He thought about what they said, about being her brothers, and this not ringing true now.

He'd been stupid to open the door, he thought, to make

it easy for them. No one visited the house; he should have thought. He would not have done so in the early days here, primed as he was for survival. The girl had made him relax, feel all safe.

He put the light on in the workshop, scanned his tools, the pile of wood. He picked up a hammer, set it down, scythed the spirit level through the air like a sword, but it was too light to do any damage. If he took the right thing upstairs, they might back down.

There was a series of dull noises and he supposed the girl was struggling with them, refusing to go. Show them there's fight in you, he thought. Like in the water.

He looked for something heavier with length, to be able to swing hard, and he must have missed the sound on the stairs because one of them was on him now, the younger one he felt, hurling them both to the wall, the boy's head striking his own again and again and he thought he would pass out. There is only one of them though, he said to himself, and he tried to find leverage on something. Like a playground fight, it became, unclean, chaotic, hardly any blows landing.

It was his own head that turned it, hard back into the boy's face, a speculative but lucky strike and he knew from the sound, from the sensation, that he'd broken the boy's nose. In the pause he turned them both over, rolled away and got to his feet. The boy was half up, but not all there, his eyes glazed, needing time to right themselves, and a heavy kick between his legs put him down again, a few more and one to the head to make sure. For a second Hallam wanted to carry on, despite it being just a boy, mostly because one of them had hurt the dog, but also because he could.

He took some deep breaths despite the pain of his lung,

178

spat a mulch of blood out. His arm had this beat to it now, palpitating with agony, and he willed the adrenaline to inundate him. A slug of something would go a long way, he knew, and he wished he'd replicated his father's custom of keeping a bottle down here.

There was more noise on the stairs and the older man was in the room now, looking pleased with himself, like he was glad it was only the two of them, this great indifference about the boy. Again Hallam glanced about, the tools near him too light or unwieldy.

Go on, the man said, try one, and the invitation of it scared him. Being allowed to go first, a free hit.

They came together more like boxers though, as if a code were to be followed, and the man got several punches in before Hallam knew about it. Jabs, like he was feeling him out, a sequence of bee stings to the face. He swung his own fist, the arm that wasn't broken, but found only air, his balance lost, and this feeling of being taunted, of knowing you were already beaten. It would be more even with less room, he thought, lunging at the man with all he had left, so it was more of a wrestle, and they went to floor.

The older man had this strength to him, more than the youngster, more than his size suggested, and he knew it was vital to find some weakness in him. They jostled for space, so their limbs could be applied, and he was glad of the confinement as he tried to use his knees. He knew this time to keep his head near the man's, so the butting was less effective, and after a few seconds he found the man's face with his hand, pushed a thumb hard into his eye socket, felt the curdled resistance of it, the ball moving around like a mussel.

A turning point, it could be, despite the man retreating

until Hallam's thumb came out, and he tried to follow it up with a series of butts, knew to go hard now.

It was strange when the man stopped struggling, as if he'd given in, or that some bell had sounded and they were to pause. A stalemate reached and the need for dialogue after all. Or that the man had passed out from all the butting, an end of sorts.

There was this realisation of something, but he didn't know what, only that when he rolled away, he saw the grin on the man's face, and that he had this blade.

He was relieved by the pause in things, found he could observe himself, as if from above. I should be panicked, he thought, but if anything there was this calmness, a softening of the dream's edges. Something like pain, he thought, different though, and he felt the need to sleep, to furl up in a corner.

He tried to recall why they had been fighting, realised he was shaking. The temperature seemed to quickly fall, as if they were outside now, as if all the walls had suddenly been removed. Think, he said to himself. What do you need to do?

The older man stood, wiped the blade on his jeans, put it away like it had been decisive. He went to the younger one, nudged him with a boot and the boy groaned, as if he was drunk. Turning to Hallam the man shook his head, like this could all have been avoided, yet at the same time there was satisfaction in him.

Was she worth it? the older man said, and Hallam tried to understand the question. The girl, he remembered, that's why they were here.

There was something left, he thought, that he could do, and he shuffled the few feet to the door, pushed it shut with the part of him that still worked and turned the key. He could sense the man coming, knew he had one go, no more, and grabbing the hatchet from the wood pile he struck the back of it hard onto the key so that it broke off.

There was another kick, a stamp to his back, and he slumped down, turned to see the older man looking at him, some of his cockiness gone, his eye bloodshot, like a bruised tomato.

That's it, he thought. We are in this space now for a while, like cellmates, and he tried not to think about the bleeding the man had given him with the blade. The three of them in this cliffside cavity and the myriad tracks their lives had run on to deliver them here. He thought of all the different kinds of person in the world and wondered which he was.

He stayed down now, let his head settle on the stone floor. The remnant of the sculpture he'd started for the girl caught his eye from the woodpile, had held its basic essence, and he could see now its potential, this avian abstraction. Why hadn't he continued with it? He was always so quick to give up on things, wondered where stamina came from. Again there was the compulsion to sleep, it being something to fight against, and yet there was no reason to.

He remembered tomorrow, knew it important not to let them down on the boat, that he'd never be asked again if he did. In the end you became as people regarded you.

This house, he thought. That it should end here, in the spine of it. Despite its neglect he had cared for it, was in some way its custodian. He'd tried to preserve it, warm it, but like the sandcastles he and Blue once made in its shadow, Seafield would always be enfeebled by the sea.

AFTER A WHILE the older man started to prowl the room, inspecting the hatch at the far end, trying the old handle, but it had long seized up. He picked up a screwdriver and worked in a frenzy at the edges, at the hinges, the wood splintering until finally the small door buckled open, the sea air a beautiful thing as it came, the breeze a lament. He watched the man look out into the night and contemplate it all, felt the weakness start to overwhelm him. Small breaths were all he could manage, barely any depth, like something in hibernation.

A few moments later the man took his jacket off and wriggled awkwardly out through the opening and was gone.

There was a coming and going, and he fought for more lucidness. How long had he been here, like this? He could hear the moaning of the other one, the boy, and bits of it came back. There was this anger in him now at the violation, which he knew could be used, like when the girl was in the sea.

He crawled to the hatchway, let the brackish notes rouse him, the sea this singular thrum, soughing onto him. He leaned out, peered into the gloom, but there was no one below. He adjusted his body, turned his head upwards, could just make out the older man scaling the cliff, the garden perhaps a dozen feet above him.

He gazed down again, remembered Blue calling up to him

that day. It was possible, he thought, if you were careful, even with the injuries. You never knew what was possible.

The hatch was barely wider than him and he had to sheath himself through it a little at a time, like a birth, and this need to both push himself out and to hold on. If your shoulders got through, he knew, the rest could.

You can do this, he said, his brother shouting up encouragement too, telling him he just needed to get some footholds, work out where all the clefts were. Don't rely too much on your arms, Blue said, the legs too were important. And you didn't need to go straight up if sideways was better. All this he knew.

He manoeuvred onto the half-ledge, swivelling his body round, holding the frame of the hatch with his good hand, wind all the time gusting him, trying to usher him back in. Looking up he could just make out the form of the older man heaving himself up over the edge, flecks of shingle falling on to him.

A moist warmth radiated out from his midriff, and for a moment he felt invincible. Knew he had it in him to finish this thing if he could catch the man.

Again the wind, spiked with brine. His fingers felt too stubby to find the ridges, inside him the loosened rib like its own dagger. Fifteen feet is all it was, perhaps eighteen. If one person had done it, he thought.

The fall seemed without start, as if it had always been happening, and he could not remember a time unfalling. Such silence, as if the world had tilted and his place in it was being long considered. And despite falling, some part of him seemed to rise – bowels, gut, heart, he couldn't tell – but a definite lurch upwards, a protest.

You have to just go with it now, he thought.

The darkness seemed to accumulate on him, like mist, and it was no unpleasant thing, a sort of anaesthesia on the path to sleep. All the sounds had coalesced, dimmed as if retreating together, gull and sea and wind, now braided beyond distinction. He sensed the girl's absence from the house, hoped she was far enough away from the man, her ankle sustaining a canter into the village and beyond. He had this fantasy, that the dog had gone with her, its instinct for survival beyond sentiment. You never really owned anything, he thought. The girl a comet, streaking through.

He had bought her some time, at least, and there was comfort in this, his own life finally of some worth.

He imagined someone finding him, the strange arrangement of his body, flung on the rocks like wrack, sandhoppers busy around him. As his mother had been. Or there would be a tide before anyone passed, and he'd be gently raised, sluiced into it and carried out into the bay, over the submerged forest.

There was breath left in him, but not much, and he felt he could cease it at any time, the decision his own. Half-life, if that, he thought, just a sequence of vibrations now, the major systems of him shutting off. Powering down, like Blue.

If there was injustice in what had happened, he didn't feel any.

The cold was absolute, colder than in the water the other evening, the heat of life dispersing from his wound. Did any of this energy survive him, he wondered. This voltage. Not necessarily a spirit, more that he knew the universe neither created nor distinguished energy, that it merely was. Wouldn't the essence of him, every wave of every particle, simply be reordered in the universe? Death this great illusion.

He tried to move a little, to arc further into the barnacled cavity he lay across, so it was like a hammock. There should be more pain, he thought, and as he did there was nothing but pain, pulsing in emphatic sweeps until something overrode it and he was able to bear it again.

He felt down to where the wound was, knew it was hopeless.

Time had laboured during the fall, just a little longer than it was supposed to, and he'd waited for the ground to rise and meet him. Two seconds of flying and something beautiful in this after all, as if he were in the woods again with his brother, time folding back on itself like the tide.

I'll get help, he kept saying again and again to Blue that day, knowing somewhere in him that it was all beyond this. What he'd wanted to say, if he could have found the courage, was: I will stay by you, so you are not alone for this. In the end he ran, not to get help, but to flee death.

And if there was a regret now, it was that no one was with him, to shepherd him. The sea perhaps, and he tried to hear it. The sea is with you.

Despite the blackness he was able to project his brother's face onto some screen in his mind, saw that big grin of his at their shared demise, like he was copying Blue. A fate of sorts.

Two seconds of falling, and your whole life in these, he thought. Like an audit. All the known and all the unknown things.

He was able to picture his mother scything through the surf, buoyant, a crop of the sea. Saw again the girl in water and this time being there for her.

And then nothing.

ACKNOWLEDGEMENTS

PARTICULAR GRATITUDE FOR this one to Ríona, whose passion for and belief in the book was both unceasing and infectious. To Felicia for helping me fall in love with Romania. To Paul Northcott for shining a light on the horrors of people-trafficking. To Jim and Si for yanking my head above the waves when needed. To Miriam for friendship and the loan of Dill. And to H. E. for the lockdown-busting swims etc.

This book has been typeset by
SALT PUBLISHING LIMITED
using Neacademia, a font designed by Sergei Egorov
for the Rosetta Type Foundry in the Czech Republic. It
is manufactured using Holmen Book Cream 70gsm, a
Forest Stewardship Council™ certified paper from the
Hallsta Paper Mill in Sweden. It was printed and bound
by Clays Limited in Bungay, Suffolk, Great Britain.

CROMER
GREAT BRITAIN
MMXXI